John Rickards Mozley

The Romance of Dennell

A Poem in Five Cantos

John Rickards Mozley

The Romance of Dennell
A Poem in Five Cantos

ISBN/EAN: 9783337049508

Printed in Europe, USA, Canada, Australia, Japan

Cover: Foto ©Andreas Hilbeck / pixelio.de

More available books at **www.hansebooks.com**

THE ROMANCE OF DENNELL

A POEM IN FIVE CANTOS

BY

JOHN RICKARDS MOZLEY

LONDON

KEGAN PAUL, TRENCH & CO., 1, PATERNOSTER SQUARE

1885

TO

MY EVER DEAR SON,

WHO DURING THIS PRESENT LIFE

IS HIDDEN FROM THE SIGHT OF THE EYES

OF ME AND MINE.

CONTENTS.

—◆◇◆—

CANTO I.

DENNELL AND HELEN.

THE ROMANCE OF DENNELL.

WHAT see'st thou in the woodland, through the covers ?
  The chequered light and shade,
The rabbit playing, the hawk o'erhead that hovers ;
  But not the woodland maid.
   Yet be but strong enough,
   Look thou but long enough,
Thou'lt find her at last, when the game is played.

There is a secret glen in Westmoreland ;
The mountains nurse it in their lap, and fence
With barriers of dense thicket and huge rock
Their darling solitude from peopled plains,
Road, farm, and cultured crop, that spread below.
A gentle torrent 'mid the flowery sward
Eddies, and kisses with his spray the fern
And wild geranium rooted 'mid the stones ;
Then with a fiercer rush he plunges down
Into the gorge engirt with craggy gloom,

Where, lost to view, his voice is hoarsely heard
Battling with stony guards for liberty.
But as you upward wend, the silence grows ;
For now it is the height of summer noon ;
The veilless sun in cloudless azure rides ;
No sound is heard, save rippling waterbreaks,
Or grasshopper that chirps among the grass,
Or where, afar, the cushat's note profound
Is softly sent from ivied woodland's night.

Lo ! by a stone in that fair wilderness,
A maiden.   In her hand the limning brush
Is token of the task she plies ; but now
The sketch forgotten on the grass is laid ;
She stands, and on the wave-washed boulder lays
Her careless arm ; some fancy, never told,
Parts with a smile the roses of her lips ;
Is it of home, or of the circling hills,
Or of some rarer and remoter thing,
She dreams ?   Whate'er it be, 'tis happiness ;
Where all is lovely, loveliest she of all.
Her hat has fallen ; an oak o'er-canopies
Her flowing hair with broad and leafy shade.

What youth is this that up the cloven gorge
Clambers from ledge to ledge with wary foot,
Propping his steps upon a hazel staff,
From whence the tender leafage scarce is shorn ?
He bears a basket, and his quick eye seeks
What rare or graceful plant or fern may lurk

Within the crannies of the precipice ;
Anon he loosens some rock-clasping root
With strong but gentle pull.   Ascending thus,
He wins the open vale at last, and sees
The maiden in her musing solitude ;
Till, half ashamed of idleness perchance
(The more in presence of a stranger's eye),
She sits, the unfinished labour to renew.
But he within a moment's fleeting space
Had caught the image of her soul, and drew
Nearer, and thus with fearless word began :
" Maiden most fair, how like a queen you sit
" Here in your realm, this solitude of hills !
" And mountain peak and glen confess your sway ;
" For now, I see, they breathe beneath your hand
" In pictured semblance of their very selves."
" Flatter me not," the maiden answering cried ;
" Nor look too long, or you will see too well
" The faults that now you miss."   But he with speed:
" You wrong your art, and know not how it seems
" Like nature's self in fair simplicity.
" Ah, and what treasure must enfolded lie
" In that portfolio ! gladly would I see,
" Did but your favour kindly grant it so——"
So saying, he 'gan draw a picture forth,
And she as quickly laid her hand to stay
The sudden theft ; so in the strife of wills
The sketch was torn across the breadth half-way.
" Take it," she cried, and left it in his hand ;
But gathering up the rest rose suddenly,

And lightly overstepped the brook, and looked
Backward with laughing eye, and thus pursued
Her chiding with a gentle irony :
" Farewell, kind sir ; I leave to you the field,
" The trophy, and the honours of the day."
"O pardon me," the youth remorseful cried ;
" What rude and sacrilegious touch was mine !
" What have I marred ! yet let me not repent,
" As now I must, if I should know you driven
" By fault of mine from this your chosen seat.
" See, I will sit, nor stir a finger more."
" Fair words ! " she said ; " but deeds have surer sound.
" You would demand, although you feign to ask ;
" How know I you will show me courtesy ?
" I trust you not ; your look is masterful."
" How can I answer for my look ? " he said.
" My mind desires not to be masterful,
" But only sitting here at peace to watch
" Your pencil's subtle motion as it blends
" Colour with colour, line with line ; and then
" Perhaps to mingle pleasant talk the while,
" Whatever rises foremost in our thought,
" To suit the sunny air and cheerful time,
" And babbling of the water by our side."
" 'Twere dangerous," the maid replied ; " for see,
" You know it not, but I have magic arts ;
" It may be, I shall cast on you a spell,
" That shall imprison you for ever here."
" That chance I'll risk," he answered hardily ;
" And, maiden, look, I hold a pledge of yours ;

" Ay, more than one ; this comely ribboned hat,
" Your fine soft brush, and colours bright as gems.
" What is the price you will redeem them for ? "
" I name no price," she cried, " for what is mine ;
" Did I not say that you were masterful ?
" And now you show that what I said was true.
" You think, because it chances you have found
" The heron's nest, the heron's self is caught ;
" Which is not so ; nor all your skill will serve
" To find her, saving with her own free will."
Up the green bank, like heron on the wing,
She fled, but ere the bushes screened her flight,
Glanced once behind ; and now he stood alone.
Swift to the race ! the bank's high crest he won,
And saw the silvan glade before him stretch,
Sloping and rising, full of tall fair trees ;
The heat lay on the sward, and all was still,
Save that, in royal purple deeply dyed,
One butterfly went slowly fluttering past,
So nigh, he could have caught it in his hand ;
It had delayed him other times, perchance ;
Not now.   Through many a covert on he ran,
Where densest boughs left scanty space o'erhead,
And ever looked, and still he looked in vain ;
Nor from the bare far-gazing hill was aught
Revealed of fluttering dress or glancing form ;
Baffled he stood, but idly cast at length
His eyes upon the sketch, his hand retained—
" Helen Dundas " was written underneath.
" O who is this ? " unto himself he said ;

" The daughter of my father's friend, whom I
" For the long space betwixt new moon and new
" Have shunned against my duty'; for I said,
" Leaving my home, that I would seek his roof,
" And bear my father's greetings to his ear ;
" Wherein I yet have failed, accounting it
" A profitless dull task, that might be shelved
" From day to day; O had I better known !
" For now I have with double rudeness marred
" The favour that belonged to me of right;
" Doubly discourteous must I seem to her ;
" Howe'er her gentleness might pardon me
" For the first fault, the second makes me seem
" A churl, unmannered.   Fool that I have been !
" Neglect is worse than open wrong."   Thus he,
Self-chiding, roamed through thicket and by stream ;
And in this mood it so befell he passed
The spot wherein the maiden hidden lay ;
She heard the words wherein he styled himself
Discourteous and a fool ; she saw his look
Of shame and trouble ; now she pitied him,
And slipping through the bushes, reached the spot
Where first she stood.   He came along the marge
Beside the waters : she to him began
With gentle words but subtle merriment :
" Forgive me, that I sent you such a chase.
" Did you desire it, you have won the right
" To see my art's poor lineaments—and yet
" They are, in truth, a learner's task, no more ;
" But rather let me tell what more will aid

"The search your basket shows; I know the haunt
"Of bright marsh-mallow, and where the royal fern,
"Flowering, is dewed by darkling torrent's spray."
Now, as she ended, with such friendliness
Of voice she touched his ears, so soft a glance
Shone in her eyes, so trustful all her mien,
That then his heart conceived the seed of love;
And had he dared, he would have clasped her hands,
And ta'en his fill of gazing on her face;
But now he held desire in check, and spoke:
"Maiden, your kindness has forgiven much;
"But I have trespassed further than you know.
"This is your name, I doubt not, written here?
"My own is Harry Dennell; I was charged
"To see your father; great is my neglect,
"Who a full month have worn away with friends,
"And still have left my father's bidding vain.
"Now do I see how great my loss has been
"Through this my fault, which I would fain repair,
"If 'tis allowed me still."　Then answered she:
"My father journeys now away from home;
"But come to-morrow; he returns ere noon;
"And gladly he will welcome you; for oft
"He names your father, counting him a friend
"Among the oldest and the best esteemed."
And saying this, she took anew the brush
And those bright colours, and began to touch
The unfinished page; he lingered by her side,
And she forbade him not; so, half with talk
And half in silence, passed an hour away.

And when the time was come that they should part,
She gave her hand; he clasped it, and his touch
And sudden look sent through her heart a thrill,
Almost of fear.   So with a wondering thought,
As if a dream had swiftly risen and fled,
A dream in strangeness, but immovable,
In texture as of firm reality,
They parted from each other's sight and voice ;
Yet sight and voice had echo manifold
Within their several souls, until the hour
When sleep and night encompassed them around.

The fisher's net drew up of old
    A vessel strong and sealed,
Within whose brazen massy fold
    A Genius lay concealed ;

But to my feet life's ocean-tide
    Has washed a crystal urn ;
What colours mantle o'er its side !
    What flashes through it burn !

O, at my touch, thou wondrous fire,
    Thy shadowing veil remove,
And pour on this wild-winged desire
    The answer of thy love !

Ere the thin crescent of the moon had filled,
Ere the great sun twice seven times had sent
The dawn, his herald, o'er the sleeping world,
The youth had said, " I love ; " the maid, " I will."
Then did they meet within that hidden glen,
Knowing that each should find the other there,
And he began :
     " O Helen ! happy hour !
" Now all things smile—all nature, and all men.
" Did never summer shine so fair as this ;
" Did never hills so sweetly open forth
" Their bosoms' secret place for dear discourse ;
" Was never face so full of life and love
" And truth as thine ; and I, more fortunate
" Than any man since Adam ope'd his eyes
" On her he loved in Eden's greenery."
And thus she answered :
      " Harry, it is strange
" I had so little heard your name before
" Chance brought us here together ; better far
" That it was so ; for thoughts of common things
" Encompass one we hear much spoken of ;
" You came about me as from lands unknown,
" Your nameless self stirred me to wondering,
" And my first glimpse of you was all my own,
" Unmarred by ruder sight.   But tell me now ;
" What hitherto has been your way of life ?
" I am assured it has been good and true ;
" But gladly I would learn the lineaments."
" Helen," he answered, "would that I could say

" I merited your praise ; but 'tis too true,
" That blame, not praise, I have deserved till now.
" My clue to life has been so scant, so torn,
" I am ashamed to speak of it to you.
" Careless amid much teaching I have been ;
" 'Twould puzzle me to say what I had done
" That is worth naming ; save I have not been
" Envious, I trust, nor grudged a friend his praise,
" Nor thought of any as my enemy.
" But shortly will my father summon me
" To share his toil ; he has great merchandise
" In many lands, and travels oft and far,
" And knows the tongues of Spain and Portugal,
" Ay, and of eastern climes ; Biscayan hills
" Yield him their deep-sunk iron ; Italian skies
" Foster the soft cocoon of glossy silk
" To swell his cargo ; tall Norwegian pines
" Are hewn for him and from the forest glens
" Whirled by the swollen flood, when blush of spring
" Dissolves the mountain snow : thence hurrying down
" O'er ledge and foaming cataract oceanward,
" Till piled at last, in even order ranged,
" They seek some English mart across the wave.
" In all my boyhood ever did I long
" To join the world of men ; but keener now
" The pulse that in me throbs, the life that springs
" To action, quick with myriad-blossomed hope."
Then Helen with a fervent voice replied :
" Ah, and the blossom of your hope shall turn
" To fruits of honour ! would that I myself

"Could follow with my brain, as with my heart,
" In all that you shall purpose ; but I fear
" The weakness of all faculties I own,
" And that I lack the grace, the strength of those
" Trained by the world's fine culture." " Nay," he cried,
" Thou shalt not fear it, Helen ! there is none
" For grace, for courage, that can pair with you.
" Heard I not from that shepherd, how you clomb
" Yon dizzy crag, and saved, one freezing morn,
" A bleating lamb, left starving, desolate ?
" Who sees you and admires not ?   O sweet soul,
" The spirit of that beauty which is yours
" Came not from elements of earth ; when stars
" Are changed in heaven, and continents dissolved
" By wasting waters, shall not this endure ?
" Shall we not love, O Helen, evermore ? "

She sat upon a mossy stone the while ;
He knelt before her suddenly, and kissed
Her hand, and then her glowing lips ; but she
Bent downward, and with bright downfalling locks
Covered his face. Of time or outward things
They held no count in that entrancing hour ;
The streamlet's rush, the song of birds, the hum
Of dragonfly borne whizzing through the air,
They felt but heard not ; so is Love's first touch,
As the first cadence of a symphony,
Itself alone in mastery supreme,
Whereto all harmonies are gathered in
With growing time, as faithful ministers
Serving their king.

At last she rose, and drew

Deep breath, and looked upon the circling hills
With eyes fresh as a child's ; and he with her.
They walked in silence for a while, and then
Dennell anew : " Helen, I have a fear
" That I displeased your father yesterday
" By a light foolish word I spoke in scorn
" Of men who pore and reason without end ;
" He seemed to take the meaning for himself,
" And looked upon me sternly.   He is deep,
" I know, in thinking.   Did I anger him ?
·· Much were I grieved if he were hurt thereby."

" O Harry, think not you have angered him
" Save for a moment ; no, nor even at all.
" But to yourself I would impart the fear
" I feel concerning him ; he is of late
" Absorbed in silent thought, and oft appears
·· Gloomy and harassed, or at rarer times
" Too keen in exultation.   'Tis three years
" Since he resigned his ancient way of life.
" He was of purpose strong and practical,
" And ruled his wealth, and ruled the wills of men ;
" Many obeyed him ; yet for all his toil
" And daily tasks he ne'er forgot me then.
"He watched me through my childhood with such care
" As from my very soul I thank him for ;
" Brother or sister I have none, and she,
" My mother, died, alas ! when I was born ;
" My father was the world to me.   How oft

" Among the woods he taught me, or at home
" When twilight's gentle calm was merged in night,
" And lamps were lit, discussing men or books
" Or nature.   But 'tis long since this has been ;
" Some eager quest engages him ; I fear
" He wastes his strength, pondering by day and night."
And Dennell answered, " May it yet be well !
" I needs must honour him."

Onward they went
To where a rock-encircled pool received
A waterfall.   Then Dennell spied a spray
Of honeysuckle falling from a crag.
He leapt upon a jutting ledge and broke
One tendril off ; into the pool it fell ;
He drew it thence glistening with waterdrops,
And gave it her ; she twined it in her hair.
The wave, that as with smiles had rippled o'er,
Calmed itself to a mirror once again,
And drew their eyes to meet far down within.
" Lo, what a second heaven is sphered," he said,
" Like sapphire in the setting of sharp crags,
" And, in their very semblance, ferns and flowers ;
" And there that underworld's sweet soul are you.
" Helen, were this the Egyptian's glass, that tells
" The fates of men, what image should we see ?
" I have been happy all my life till now ;
" Father, and mother, and a sheltered home,
" A sister's dear companionship, are mine ;
" And now the crowning hour, the summer rose,
" The very sunburst of all bliss has shone !

"Is this too strange to last ?   Men say, the world
"Is full of evil ; will it sometime reach
"Ourselves ?   O hark !   I hear a thunderous sound
"Low on the horizon ; some would say, the skies
"Murmured an answer.   Well, befall what may,
"We will be brave in hope."

                          But Helen cried,
"Vex not yourself with troublous thought to-day !
"What can we think of now, but this pure eve,
"So beautiful in earth, air, waters, woods ?
"To-day to us is like eternity ;
"'Tis our possession ; never can it fade ;
"This happy time is safe and garnered in,
"And none can ever wrest it from us now.
"And think you not the birds and breathing flowers,
"And even the beck and rocks and fragrant pines,
"Rejoice with us and love us, as we love
"Each other ? "

                So they talked, until the glen
Was deep in shade, and topmost peaks alone
Glowed with the redness of the setting sun.

          O golden sun, O happy day,
          Why hasten, hasten thus away?
          A little while, a little while,
          A little longer on us smile.

          Dark-vestured queen, so soon must thou
          With starry circle wreathe thy brow?

O Night, anon thou'lt welcome be,
When he I love is gone from me.

Is it the star of Love that shines
Between yon cloudy western lines?
O star untrue, that giv'st command
To sever loving hand from hand !

When he I love from me is gone,
And in my chamber all alone
I loose the honeysuckle spray
He culled to deck my hair to-day ;

The fragrance still shall breathe him nigh
In dreams, as on my bed I lie ;
In dreams with him I'll wander o'er
The mountain side, the lake's still shore.

But now there is no need to dream ;
We sit beside the bubbling stream ;
O Night, a little while delay !
O linger yet, wan fading Day !

Alas, they hear not ; sad and slow
The west puts off her crimson glow ;
The night winds gather bleak and chill,
Larger in darkness looms the hill,
And louder sounds the rushing rill.

C

December's gloom is here.   The black north-east
Sweeps cloudy squadrons through the chilling air ;
Above, all motionless they seem to lie,
Lords of the rayless heaven from pole to pole,
From east to sullen west.   The leafless woods
Bend in the blast ; dark, iron bound the earth.

And Helen in her chamber sat, and mused :
" O what shall be the issue ?   Let me seek
" The clue to solve these doubts.   Five weeks are gone
" Since from his own hand first the tidings came
" Calamitous, how all his father's wealth
" Tottered to falling, and that honoured name
" Would stand a mark for shafts of idle tongues ;
" That this was certain ; Ruin's crashing knell
" Would sound next day at morn ; nor could he know
" What help or helplessness should be in store
" For him and his ; and further he pursued :
" 'Take counsel, dearest Helen, what is best ;
" 'What grief, what sin, were I to mar your days !
" 'There can be no decision from your tongue
" 'But what I will approve with all my soul.'
" Then answered I, ' Have courage ; I did ne'er
" 'Limit my promised faith to prosperous hours ;
" 'I faint not now.   Yesterday was blue sky ;
" 'To-day, a storm ; so Nature's courses change.
" 'The haven of our rest, that erst we hoped
" 'To reach before another year was born,
" 'Is now a little further from us set ;
" 'But we will gain it still.   Yet when time serves,

" ' How gladly would I see you and talk o'er
" ' These troubles ; writing is as nought to speech.'
" Alas ! I knew not at that hour the worst——— "
Now from the casement did she cast her eyes
Downward ; and lo ! upon the woodland path
Hard by, with eager glances upward turned,
Was he of whom she thought.   Then stayed she not
A moment's space, but ran and met him there ;
With haste he cried, " Not here ! " as she drew nigh ;
" Come, follow me ; we need a secret place."
He led the way to where a hollow sunk
Delved in the woodland, sheltered from the wind ;
There hollies grew, and withered bracken still
In early winter made a pleasant couch.
Thereon they sat apart, and he began :
" Helen, it does not need to tell of grief ;
" Trouble is round us, in us ; but though ne'er
" My voice should speak hereafter to thine ear,
" Now must we tell the current of our souls.
" Your father bids us tear our mutual bond ;
" And from the hour his strict command was sent,
" You have been silent."   " Harry, I am true,"
Swift with impetuous speech the girl broke in ;
" Ah, did he write to you ?   I knew it not.
" If I was silent, hear the cause.   You wrote
" Unto myself, that you would shortly come :
" Scarce had I read those words, that very hour
" My father entered ; anger fiercely glowed
" Upon his face, his accent, harsh and strange,
" Sounded diverse from all I ever heard.

" Preface was none ; he bade me take the pen
" And write eternal severance on our love.
" O me, what fear was mine ! lest I some ill
" Should work him, disobeying ; for it seemed
" As if his passion must have vent in act,
" Or strike itself with pangs of fierce recoil ;
" And when amid such tumult I at last
" Gathered the cause, that we were stricken too
" And shaken by your ruin, that seemed light
" Beside the terror that I felt for him.
" Natheless, I would not yield ; no, not a whit.
" O no ; my faith, my heart, my hope, are yours."

" O pardon, if a moment I could doubt !
" Say on, my Helen."
                              " Then he pressed me more ;
" Said, like all women, I could doubtless feign
" Obedience, love, respect, yet all the while
" Dissembling my true will.   It touched my heart,
" That he should think I hid my soul from him !
" I promised he should know my every act.
" O Harry, I have watched through many a night,
" And from my casement seen the stars go round,
" And great Orion stalk across the sky,
" My bed untouched till morning, while I thought,
" Shall I keep silence longer ? shall I trust
" That you would come?   And you have come ; and now
" We know each other."   Dennell then again :
" What forecast, Helen, hold you in your mind ? "
" Harry, 'tis given us to love ; but mark,

"Weigh well the price that we for love must pay.
"Not, as the wont of lovers is, and ours
"In happier days has been, by sight and touch,
"By written word and spoken, look and sign,
"That told what others knew not, must we love ;
"No, but in absence and by silent trust ;
"The seed of bliss beyond our eager sense ;
"The bitter juice of unaccomplished hope
"Marring the pleasant wine of youth's desire ;—
"This must I bear for you, and you for me.
"Shall I be joyful, when my father's pain
"Weighs thus upon him?   We must wait awhile,
"Refraining converse when to-day is o'er.
"And, Harry, time works change in many things ;
"My father's wrath will soften ; he will look
"Again upon your face with kindliness ;
"And you will prosper in life's ways, and nought
"Of all these clouds will last in memory."

"Helen, your words are full of truth and love ;
"Yet listen.   I must cross the Atlantic deep ;
"In far Brazil henceforth my life must lie ;
"There only have I found an honest work,
"Refused by those who erst had called me friend.
"O how can we endure, so far apart,
"To be without a token, sign, or word?
"I may be fixed in poverty, or die
"Unheard of ; how will you expectant watch
"The pale and creeping years that steal away
"Your beauty's peerless flower ; while I, entombed,

" Should be the foe that drained your life ! "

She wept ;

" Is this, then, needful ?   If 'tis so indeed,
" As each year passes, when the sun of June
" Reaches his height upon our English shore,
" You shall by letter tell me of your lot,
" And I will, answering, tell of mine in turn."
" 'Tis well," he answered.   " Helen, tell me now,
" How great is your disaster, bred from ours ?
" Last night I had a dream of pain ; methought,
" Barefoot I wandered over rough lone hills,
" And voices through the air came whispering
" That you were dead, and I had murdered you ;
" I see even now the blood upon the stones.
" But mine, or yours ? "

She smiled, and answering said :

" Dear dreamer, dream not so ; 'tis mere unrest.
" We know not yet our sum of loss ; at least,
" Not beggary, nor even loss of home ;
" Console yourself thus far ; but yet the chill
" Of disappointment strikes my father deep
" To the heart's core.   Long-cherished plans were his,
" Which to accomplish needed help of gold ;
" Now they are left as airy palaces
" Within his visionary brain ; he broods
" Ever upon the past ; I weep for him."
Then Dennell rose.   " I go to see him, Helen."
" Ah, wherefore?   You will fall to bitter strife."
" Can I accept the sentence he has passed,
" Not ratified by you?   Nay, I must say,

"What is plain truth, that I abide your lover,
"Lest he should say hereafter that deceit
"Lay in my silence ; trust me, I will ne'er
"Prolong discussion with renewed offence ;
"And for his scorn and anger, Helen, know,
"They shall be like a doctor's bitter draught,
"That strengthens more than wine."

                  " If go you must,
"O say not more than needful ! See, I'll wait
"In the side alley, where our shrubbery
"Touches this wood ; come there, when all is done."

Now Helen's father in his chamber sat,
Beside the fire with blazing logs up-piled,
That shone the cheerier for the outer cold ;
A little man white-haired, of thin worn face,
But high and massive brow, that seemed to know
The things it did despise ; his lips were keen,
His glance direct and firm, as used to rule,
And yet a languor seemed to rest on him.
Feebly he moved, as if oppressed with care ;
Or sat and pondered, head upon his hand
Supporting ; or surveyed the grey dull scene,
The garden withering fast in sere decay,
The darkening sky and wintry afternoon,—
Till Dennell entered. Sudden energy
Braced then the old man's mien ; erect he stood,
All heed, and with a silent keen regard
Scanned piercingly the youth, who thus began :
"Deep is my grief, that in the fatal wreck

" That has o'erwhelmed our fortunes utterly,
" You too are harmed. I may not cover o'er
" My acts in silence, seeing that yourself
" Have in your daughter such dear interest,
" As truly you did write to me erewhile.
" Sir, I have ever honoured you ; and yet
"Think not I am unmindful of your will,
" If I should say, your daughter's voice is that
" Which must command me in this troublous day ;
" Her faith in me I may not disavow."
Then with a bitter smile Dundas replied :
" The phantasies of youth o'ercloud your brain.
" Heaven guard my daughter from such faith as I
" Had in your sire ! the glittering web is torn ;
"No hand shall piece the shreds together now."
" Could you but see my father," Dennell cried,
" You would forgive, so grievous is his pain."
But darker grew the face of old Dundas.
" Use not soft words.   Can you undo the wrong
" That strikes more deep than your mind's fathoming?"
Then Dennell answered : "Say you, when ourselves
" Are brought to ruin, utterly cast down,
" Your lighter suffering is unfathomable ?
" My father fell not through dishonour's stain,
" But from ambition ; is his penalty
" Less than his fault, in scales of justice weighed?"
With double scorn Dundas sent back reply :
" Why, I am forced to yield.   Come, let us live
" Together, brethren in adversity ;
" Your father, mother, sister, and yourself

" With my unworthy self ; such worthy guests
" Will pardon, if my board is straitened now."
" Alas ! you mock me." " True, my mood would scarce
" Suit with your father ; he is honourable,
" So you have said.   It may be so ; men say
" That there is honour among thieves ; but I
" Am stinted in such honour."   Dennell cried
With anger hot : " O heart of cruelty !
" What ! came I hither, suffering all in soul,
" To hear such falsehood and such proofless gibe ?
" 'Tis thy inhuman selfishness that prompts
" These taunting words : ne'er knew I thee till now."

Now, as he spoke, was Helen straying near ;
For up and down with fevered pulse she went,
Torn by the crowd of restless thoughts ; or else
Her eye would glance upon some casual thing
Beside her footstep—weed or tangled shrub,
Or poor pale rosebud out of season born,
By bleak December frozen from the life
Wherewith it longed to grace the light of heaven :
So straying did she hear the wrathful sound
Of voices as in strife ; she hastened then.
As Dennell ended, swiftly, silently,
The door was opened ; one did enter in ;
He turned not, for he knew her.   She no glance
Cast upon aught within the room, but seized
Her father's hand, and spoke with streaming eyes :
" O pardon him, my Harry, standing here !
" See, is there treachery upon his face ?

"You will not say it ; dulness? no, nor sloth ;
"But brave endeavour, and true honesty.
"Calamity itself will be his strength,
"From whence with suppler nerve he will arise,
"As doth a swimmer from the briny sea.
"O try him ; he will aid, not injure you ;
"I am a girl, and yet methinks I know
"What marks a man that can endure and win."
Then first in gentler tone the old man spoke,
For much he loved his daughter : "Helen, child,
"What judge are you of men ?   Young sir, attend.
"My words against your father (I am frank)
"Flew in their haste beyond the mark.   Natheless
"Your presence pleases not.   Remind me not
"Henceforth of what has been, nor dare to say
"I have approved your wooing ; that is past ;
"My anger sleeps till you revive it thus,
"Pestering my ears with tales of love, that now
"Has lost its aliment and sustenance,
"And needs must wither in this huge collapse.
"The cup of memories that you proffer me
"Is spoilt and stale and harsh to taste, like milk
"Made sour by thunder.   If you seek to win
"My daughter, you must come in wealthier guise
"Than that you show.   I pray you, leave me now ;
"My thoughts are bent on matters of great need."

So Dennell left the chamber, and awhile
Lingered, nor vainly, in the garden walks.
She came, whose face and voice so long, so long,

Light of his eyes and music to his ears
Should be desired and missed; she placed her arms
About his neck, and uttered sweet good-bye;
And then with tears they parted; and night fell.

Even as the sun draws up the dull thick cloud
   From ocean depths and hides therewith his face,
Himself the weaver of his pallid shroud,
   Himself the spoiler of his own fair grace;

So thou, O Love, with shame thyself dost veil,
   Shame born of fear, that bitter troubled deep;
O who shall know thee, poor and mute and pale?
   Men pass thee by, all vainly dost thou weep.

Thou sittest in the crowded street, alone;
   And all the people chaffer for their wares,
Rare gem or fragrant spice; of all, not one
   To speak to thee or hear or see thee cares;

Not one thy tender beauty can discern,
   Much less the fire with life's own fuel fed,
That in thy heart eternally doth burn;
   They see but folded hands and muffled head:

Wert thou to rise unveiled, how would their strife
   In silence fall; how trembling would they view
Thy face, the unshadowed joy and light of life;
   But now they deem a beggar's dole thy due.

Yet sometime shall the sun his bondage burst,
  And with a thousandfold more glory glow
On scattered clouds, that held him prisoner erst;
  And thou, O Love, be not ashamed, but know,
That which in secret silence now is nursed,
  Some day through earth and skies shall overflow.

————

Now swiftly draws the hour of exile near;
From her, who is the loadstone of his soul,
Severed by fate, he flies.   O let him still
List to the strain which Memory sings of love!
For soon the trumpet peal, that calls to act,
Must drown that siren's voice; and he in stir
And din of battle must attend alone
The nearest mark, whereto his hand is set.
O happy, if the tender chords beneath
Sound trembling through the fibres of his heart,
From whence at last the perfect melody
Shall rise above the cries of earth supreme!

Loosed is the cable, and the groaning ship
Parts from her moorings.   Through the crowded port,
Under the red-roofed houses, 'mid the stir
Of shouting sailors, while tar-laden airs
Yield to the freshening breath from ocean borne,
Into the broader space she moves, and then
Upon the open deep.   The harbour now,
With its array of masts and hulls and flags,

Receding lessens, and the cliffs expand
This way and that along the lonely shore;
Till these too sink diminished, and the far
Mountains arise, their hoar heads flecked with snow.
By touch of early spring; the mountains these
Of Devon, far from those dear Cumbrian hills,
Yet for the likeness of their cloven glens
These too are dear to Dennell, and he sits
And watches how they glitter in the morn;
There at the stern he leans his arm upon
The bulwark, silent, motionless, until
They sink behind this great globe's envious mound,
And the last trace of his own land is gone.

Now while he mutely gazes, let us mark
The company that with him sail the deep.
First paces o'er the deck with steady step
A merchant (it is plain to see)—perchance
The Consul of some far Brazilian port—
With shrewd square face and dignity of air,
Threescore of years upon his grizzled locks.
With him a dark-eyed girl; you would not err
Saying her seventeenth summer yet would shine;
Light was her motion; on her father's arm
She laid her hand, some question bent to ask.
So they passed on; and presently two youths
Together went conversing; on the face
Of one were lines that mark the student life,
And seemingly he was in feeble health,
Yet would you say he lacked not force, such force,

As, in the fiery frames that hold it most,
Wastes the possessor; and his brow was knit,
His lips were curled, as if in angry mood;
And yet it seemed not anger; in his voice
A music breathed; and now again he smiled.
" The sea grows calmer, Hardiman," he said
To the other darker youth, of sturdier frame.
" 'Tis so, Peranne," returned the other, " yet
" Look at those whirling clouds, that comet-like
" Hang in the upper azure; they will bring
" Wind, or I err, to-morrow by this time."
But now another broader-shouldered man
Stepped from the cabin, raven-haired, black-eyed,
In prime of days, and free and bold his gait;
And after him a comely woman went,
Full rounded in her lineaments, and firm
In mien and look.   She twined her arm in his;
Upon her finger shone the marriage ring.
In husbandly and wifely confidence
Talking they went, yet parted soon, and she
Plied with her hands some work of broidered hues,
Marking with clear observant eyes the while
The passing scene; he drawing near the youths,
Asked of their names, and told his own in turn—
Farquhar; and asked their end of voyaging,
And purpose.   Hardiman replied the first :
" My journey's end is that great riverflood,
" Which, where it rolls against the Atlantic main,
" Is named La Plata; stemming whose broad tide
" The sailor deems himself in ocean still,

" For either shore is hidden to the view ;
" But where the mighty branches separate flow,
" Parana, Paraguay, or Uruguay,
" A thousand pastures spread beside the wave ;
" And countless herds ; by these I hope to thrive."
And next Peranne ; in accents softer he :
" If one could tell my term of wanderings,
" More gladly should I hear than any man ;
" But who can prophesy the hour of health
" That now is far away ? for this I seek ;
" If haply briny winds may favouring bear
" Sweet ministrations with their living breath."
Then held they further converse, and Peranne
Mingled without reserve, yet presently
Withdrew insensibly from th' other twain,
As one in whom the inward eye was strong,
Immersed in meditation deep and grave.
Said Farquhar then to Hardiman : " Your friend
" Is deep in thought; a learned man belike ?"
" Ay, he is so too much, and has been nigh
" The doors of death through over-studious zeal.
" He is a man who ne'er would rest from toil;
" Keen in ambition, and of varying mood ;
" Sometimes in books immoderate, other times
" Wearing his frame with travel, for he loved
" Outlandish scenes and men ; he would prefer
" Hindoo to Christian, Turk to Englishman,
" And knew their speech, and half believed their creeds;
" So ran the tale ; but many tales are lies.
" Howe'er it be, he had no enemy,

" Though some misdoubted him ; but now I trust
" With soberer zeal he will revive to health."
"These humours," Farquhar answered, "ne'er were seen
" In any, in the parts where I was bred.
" Well, each man has his pleasure and his ill.
" Our brains were slow and steady; but we found
" Peril and pleasure on the field of chase,
" Or on the sea. Ah, 'twas a merry life ;
" 'Tis past and over : I have ta'en a part
" Experimental ; scarce I know myself.
" The most good-natured and the foolishest
" Was I among my brothers ; so they set
" (Sharing of late our common heritage)
" The least desired of all the parts to me ;
" 'Twas an estate, in uplands of Brazil,
"My mother's portion ; in her veins was mixed
" The blood of Portugal."

      As thus they talked,
Peranne went brooding on his lonely way :
" O thou mislearner of the ways of life !
" What is the thing for which thou hast o'erworn
" Brain, heart, and life, and dulled the passing hours ?
"What vain void prize, what never-sighted goal ?
" Look now at these, that are content to be
" As nature made them ; how they walk the world
" Thriving as lions ! 'tis their heritage.
"I must admire them truly. Yet, methinks,
" Somewhat they lack, some all-informing power ;
" And shall I name it—knowledge ? Ah, I sought
"For knowledge ; but 'twas chaff and husk to me ;

" And that great mark whereat my spirit aimed
" Fled from me like a ghost."

                              So murmured he :
But now upon his eyes an image fell
That met and turned his flow of sad complaint ;
For near him stood and played, with merry mien,
The dark-eyed maiden. Round her barking leaped
A little dog, in life's first tender weeks,
Uncouth, yet winning for uncouthness more.
It gambolled to his feet : stooping he took
And clasped it in his arms and gave it her ;
Their eyes just met.   She ran apart, and he
Forgot his care in gazing, while she lays
Her hand within the tiny teeth that feign
To hurt but cannot bite, and then again
Gathering the pink folds round her, flies away,
Laughing and calling to her pet, that runs
In fierce pursuit and tumbles many a time,
But ne'er o'ertakes until she wills it so
And fondles it again.   At last she rests ;
Yet stands, and gazes o'er the boundless sea ;
Peranne drew near ; she lingered where she was.
It chanced a shoal of porpoises just then
Tumbled and tossed within the briny foam.
A sight they were for those to wonder at,
Who love to see the kindred pulses play
In unfamiliar things, unused to man ;
So did they leap, and swim, and plunge, and dive,
Then in the green wave glimmering rose again ;
And one would dart before the rest, and race

                                                    D

With the good ship, and pass around her bows
In triumph, turning then to seek his mates.
"See, see," with eyes dilating and raised hand,
The girl exclaimed ; " oh, what great fish are they?
" Are they not like an army in the deep,
" And this our ship the castle in their midst,
" Which they beleaguer?   Tell me, what their name ? "
Then said Peranne, " Porpoises they are called
" And swine o' the sea, to-day ; but 'twas of such
" Men fancied once divinely, as if they
" Were steeds whereon the sea-gods sat, and blew
" Their echoing horns, just heard of wondering men
" In blithe bright hours across the sparkling waves ;
" And then their name melodiously fell,
" As dolphin named of sailor and of bard."
" Tell me of those old days,'' replied the girl ;
" How is it, now, sweet poetry has fled
" From thoughts of common men ? "
                              " Ah, who shall say ?
" 'Tis a pulsation from some heart unknown,
" Ours and not ours.   In secret is it born :
" It throbs, and all this mortal frame becomes
" A voice, and motion is as melody.
" But if you love the tales of ancient time,
" Say, heard you ever of Arion, then ? "
" Never ; I pray you tell."   And he began :
" Long, long ago upon the sea he sailed
" With treacherous mates, of ears too gross to take
" Impress of melodies divinely born,
" But eyes o'erkeen to watch his glittering gold,

" Deemed by him as a toy ; the which to gain,

" They seized and flung him overboard ; but he,

" Ere yet they did accomplish that intent,

" With earnest prayers gained one small boon, once
     more

" To strike the throbbing chords of his dear lyre.

" And what those rough souls heard but heeded not,

" A dolphin heard and felt ; the poor dumb fish

" From the far deep drew nearer at that sound,

" And as the heaven-taught master touched the waves,

" Rose up, and bore him on his swelling back.

" So did Arion o'er the ocean ride,

" And as he went, he struck the lyre anew

" In joyous rapture ; and bewilderment

" Amazed the dwellers on that foam-washed shore

" At the strange sight ; but more amazed was he

" That men should know not, than that beasts should
     know

" The o'er-mastering power to gentle music given."

" Ah, 'tis a pretty tale," she said ; but now

Her father called, " Sylvia, the air is cool ;

" 'Twere best you took a cloak against the wind."

So from Peranne she went ; but in his soul

Was born a seed of many things to come.

INTERMEZZO.

Sylvia.

Canst thou entrance the listening sky and sea
(Like him whose tale thou didst unfold to me)
With lyre and song conjoined in harmony?

Peranne.

The art once learned perchance may linger still,
My hand is ready, though but small my skill,
Maiden, to do obedience to thy will.

Sylvia.

From this guitar awake the slumbering sound;
And see, our company are gathering round
To hear and aid the pleasure we have found.

Peranne.

O days and years
So full of fears,
Who, who shall greet
Your sullen feet?

Wakes the green earth,
Wake the blue skies,
A sun-bright birth
To opening eyes;

But Sorrow soon
At height of noon
In the heart's hall
Keeps festival;

And cloudy cold
The wefts of gray
Falling enfold
The dying day.

O haste, O shine,
Maiden divine,
Aurora bright,
With quickening light

For hours unborn,
With laughing lips
For men forlorn
In night's eclipse.

LAURA.

O cool is the even, and clear is the heaven,
   As we sail to the land of the west;
The winds whisper lightly, the waves sparkle brightly,
   And blithe is the hope of our quest !

The brood of the sea in the billows are playing,
   They leap with a glittering foam;
And look where behind us a seagull is straying,
   But soon is he weary for home.

Farewell to our home! ye remembrances tender,
   Ye dear ones of childhood, farewell!
To the flame on the verge, to the beaconing splendour
   Bear onward, great deep, with thy swell.

O land of the sunset! O great riven mountains
   Whose crown is of snow and of fire!
Thou measureless woodland! ye floods and far
   fountains!
   O breathe in us noble desire!

Shall ours be the courage your strength to inherit,
   And win you to lovelier life?
Alas! but we tremble, for frail is our spirit,
   And stern is the toil and the strife:

O Earth, many teeming, thy vesture enweaving
   With living mysterious thread,
Thou callest, we hear thee, and joyous or grieving
   Our feet ever onward are sped;

As a child gone astray in the green forest mazes
   Will weep for a moment in fear,
Till lifting his head in new wonder he gazes—
   Lo! nigh him the wide-antlered deer;

A whirring of winds from the brake is ascending,
   A foxglove is clasped in his hand,
And afar through the pines with the azure is blending
   A verdurous limitless land;

By rapture of daring his spirit is holden,
    He strains to the heather-crowned height ;
For him and for us be the hours bright and golden,
    And hope be for ever our light !

DENNELL.

The glory of the opening skies
Streams on thy heavenward-gazing eyes,
The murmurs of the mighty sea
Give melody for melody ;

While in thy hand the glowing lyre
Scatters her notes, as sparks of fire
From steel and hammer's ringing strife
Rush forth to brief and burning life.

Through nerve and sense, and pulse and heart
The sweet keen arrows quivering dart ;
Joy at their touch awakes, as flowers
Bloom in the quickening April showers.

And lo ! and lo ! the king of day
Has caught the echo of thy lay ;
From rents of gloom he bears him forth,
And flashes far to east and north ;

O see, how stream his locks of gold
Through crimson clouds in tumult rolled !
But face and form are lost to sight
In that abyss of dazzling light ;

And if he be, as poets tell,
Lord of the music-breathing shell,
Has he not surely come to ask,
" Who is it steals my wonted task ? "

Then onward to his western hall
In state he glides majestical ;
In the broad flood his strength he laves ;
The song is mute upon the waves.

O lady, yet once more again
Breathe from thy lips the living strain ;
That so our dreams to-night may be
Melodious with thy lyre and thee.

LAURA.

Maiden, mistress of the lyre,
Ere appear the starry choir
    In the darkling sky,
    Ere we sink to sleep,
    Bid good-bye
To the day that melts away
    O'er the heaving deep.

SYLVIA.

Haste, O Night !
    Land and sea
    Thirst for thee !
Haste, O Night !

Dark-robed arise,
　　And with the wave
　　Of Lethe lave
Our burdened eyes.

With soft hand press
　　Till we forget
　　Fever and fret
And weariness.

Take, take away
　　The stir, the glare,
　　The busy care
Of restless day !

Haste, O Night !
　　Land and sea
　　Thirst for thee !
Haste, O Night !

———

But morning brought a fresh and boisterous wind,
As Hardiman foretold ; the sky was clad
In gray and stormy mantle, and the waves
Rose high and white, and sailors only dared
The deck ; save Conway (Sylvia's father he),
And with him Farquhar, both inured to seas
Higher and rougher, and the ship to them
Was as the earth whose revolution swift

Seems stable rest to folk that walk thereon.
And Dennell joined them soon, for in his veins
Ran vigorous blood, that shrank not but embraced
Each novel impulse ; so he loved to pace
The wave-washed planks, and from the bulwarks look
Into the trough of monstrous curling shapes,
Whose roaring seemed the cry of living things
Opening their mouths for prey.   Calamity
Not yet had brought the numbness to his heart
Most pitiable, that dulls each living sense ;
All things that are, glowed yet to his free sight.

But now the waves were calmed again, and on
With favouring breeze to ever warmer skies
They voyaged ; and more intimate discourse
From each to each grew daily, as is wont
Where nothing hinders and the time persuades.
So it befell upon a sunny day,
Peranne sat playing chess with Sylvia,
While a light wind its gentle coolness breathed,
But ruffled not the sea nor swayed the deck ;
Conway hard by with curious eyes surveyed
A ship that hailed them on the deep that morn,
And now was passing on to th' eastern verge ;
Dennell with Farquhar's wife conversed apart ;
Laura her name.   "This wholesome breeze," he said,
"Has given Peranne a colour in his cheek.
"Radiant he seems ; is this because he wins?"
"Either the game," said Laura, "pleases him,
"Or his companion.   Tell me ; yesterday

" I saw you listening, while with ardent look
" He spoke, and ever and anon thrust out
" His hands, as if emphatic in appeal,
" Or meditative glanced on sea and sky.
" What purport had his speech, if I may learn ? "
And Dennell answered : " He is one whose soul
" Is keen, perchance e'en keener than is right.
" The iniquities that grow inveterate
" Upon this earth anger him overmuch,
" Specially those wherein the world's high powers
" Are blameable ; he holds the worth of these
" But lightly.   Yet it seemed not he was prone
" To captious blame or cynic self-esteem ;
" Rather in hope extreme, exuberant ;
" He took the eagle wings of prophecy,
" And from his glowing height beheld the tree
" Of destiny send forth bough, bud, and fruit,
" To nourish and to gladden humankind
" For many a thousand year. ' Look you,' he cried,
" ' What sight is this ? what music in our ears ?
" ' What new harmonious order is built up
" ' By hands unseen ?   Ay, as Amphion bade
" ' By lyre and song the stones arise and frame
" ' The giant walls of seven-gated Thebes,
" ' So doth a rhythmic impulse move and work
" ' Within all lands and fashion them for good :
" ' Stretches not every nation hand to hand ?
" ' Whispers not tongue to tongue through all the world ?
" ' Where shall it cease, this mutual clasp, this flow,
" ' Thought gendering thought, and soul immixed with
      soul ?

"'Who sees this vision,' added he, 'has rule
"'And mastery o'er the ages yet to come.'
"He moved me by his ardour, and indeed
"I lean to loving him; he seemed as one
"Who knew the touch of trouble and was made
"Tenderer thereby; yet truly he might err.
"I know not in what manner, with what ends,
"Patience, or foresight, he will act; I fear
"The shocks of life may harm him." Laura then:
"High dreams endanger common happy life.
"If he should wish to marry?"
                              Saying thus,
She looked at Sylvia and Peranne, and crossed
(And Dennell after her) to where they sat
Lost in their playing. Sylvia cried, "Checkmate!"
But added, "'Tis but half a victory;
"For I had vantage given." To her Peranne:
"Each day your skill grows more." With that he
       turned
And cried to Laura: "Love you not this calm
"Soft-breathing weather, and this glorious sun?"
"Ay, but I also love," she said, "the wind,
"The spray upon my cheek. Full many a morn
"And noon and night have I a-fishing gone,
"And seen the great white-maned sea-horses leap
"Against the prow that pierced their surging line;
"With straining arms have rowed, to round the point
"Of perilous cliffs, 'gainst which the tempest drove."
"And where," said he, "was this?" "On Ireland's
       coast;

" There was my birthplace, there my childhood's home."
Broke in thereat old Conway's cheery voice.
" Where, Mistress Farquhar, is your husband gone ?
" I owe him for a wager yesterday ;
" He raised and held an iron bar full length
" No other man could lift."   " He ever loves,"
Said Dennell, " feats of voluntary toil.
" Methinks he now is gone with Hardiman
" To feed the furnace in the engine-room."
Even as he spoke Farquhar appeared above ;
Hardiman after him.   But Hardiman
No eye could notice, Farquhar being there ;
For Farquhar, though in common stoker's dress,
Black, rough, unkempt, his shaggy breast just shown,
Yet with his flashing eye, his mighty frame,
His huge free stride and sinewy waving arms,
Seemed rather one of those that smote the steel
In hollow Etna's caverns, and impelled
The flaming blast through bulk of rocks immense,
To scare the world of men, a giant brood ;
And haply silent he had gone aside ;
But when he saw all eyes in wonder bent
Upon him, seizing Hardiman he cried,
" See how they stare ! come, let them look their fill ! "
And with his comrade strode in front of them.
And now were bandied jests and quick replies,
A mimic war of words ; and Hardiman
Recalled a word that Farquhar had let fall
A while ago of somewhat he could tell
Touching his wife ; the rest with eager speech

Demanded they should hear the tale in full.
So in fresh raiment presently attired
Thus Farquhar spoke : " 'Tis just four years ago
" Since I, with six stout comrades, sought for sport
" Around the rocky bars of those wild seas
" That strike on Ireland from the northern pole.
" Sometimes afar from land we cast the line ;
" Sometimes in caves and cracks of seaworn cliffs
" We followed up the darkness-loving prey,
" And many a spoil and trophy brought we back.
" High were our spirits, and our purse was full ;
" Store of acquaintance everywhere was ours,
" So that the days went merrily along.
" And danger mingled, like a pinch of salt,
" To flavour each adventure.   It befell,
" One eve we had ta'en nothing all the day.
" The cliffs ran far along to right and left,
" But in the middle sank, and left a bay,
" Wherein were fisher huts ; the curling smoke
" Of inmates told, but none were seen around ;
" And on the beach were fish in stacks up-piled.
" Then one of us cried out—a wild young lad,
" With yellow curling locks and ruddy cheek—
" ' Come, let us seize one pile and bear it off,
" ' And from behind that rocky corner watch
" ' The fun when they begin to count them wrong.'
" So said, so done ; but they had seen, and rushed
" Down to the beach, a yelling furious crowd.
" Two boats they manned, and pulled in chase of us.
" We fled ; a whizzing shot with loud report

" And puff of smoke lent wings to oars that erst

" Had lacked not speed. We too were armed; but peace

" Must needs be kept, saving in last resort.

" We turned the point, and safety gained awhile.

" There was a cave up high upon the cliff,

" One narrow path, one only, led thereto ;

" So heaping seaweed on our boat with care

" To hide all trace, we sought and gained the cave.

" When next they came in sight, perplexed awhile

" They rested on their oars, but not for long ;

" Conjecture of our hiding-place was swift,

" And presently they spied us.   Then to shew

" Our preparation, I behind a rock

" Stood with the pistol to command the way,

" So that they well could see both me and it,

" Yet have but little mark if they should fire.

" But their design was diffcrent, as it seemed ;

" They held debate, and presently pulled in,

" And one alone came up the perilous track.

" ' See, 'tis a woman,' whispered one behind

" To me who held the pistol; so I turned

" The muzzle downwards.   Drawing then more near,

" She waved a handkerchief, the sign of peace ;

" And we returned the token.   Entering in

" Among us, she exclaimed : ' And you rich folk,

" ' And are you not ashamed to steal the food

" ' Which poor men win with labour and with sweat ? '

" She spoke with energy and fire, and looked

" More than she spoke ; and we, as best we might,

" Must make amends.   We parleyed with our foes ;
" And solemnized that night the new-made peace
" At supper.   Many a tale we told and heard.
" Now, should you ask the name of her, the girl
" That fearless dared to face the pistol's mouth,
     Look not far hence ; she sits before you now."

———

Sweet idleness ! thy empery is o'er ;
     Blithe hours are fled, like foam upon the sea ;
Our vessel wins to that Hesperian shore,
     Where dreams must cease, and toil begin to be.
     Yet, yet, a breathing-space is left ; O see
How nature gilds the closing of our way
     (Chiding not yet her children's liberty),
     And blends all earthly beauties in thy bay,
Rio, that quivers now 'neath morn's awakening ray !

———

" Land ho ! " 'twas cried ; night lay upon the sea.
Through the strait portals flies the eager ship,
'Twixt guarding heights on either hand scarce seen,
To the bosom of that fair lake far withdrawn,
Whose dim mysterious tremblings darkly show
A bride's pure soul ; and whom doth she await ?
Lo ! suddenly he comes ; he doth not stay,
When once his burning heart is set to move,
But rising from his eastern hall he greets

Her deep abounding flood with love and light ;
How like a conqueror beats he back the night,
Not lingering in long dalliance with the foe,
But winning all at once the fields of air !
And she, his peerless queen, exulting now
In the fulfilment of her dear desire,
Lays all her treasures out to mortal eye.
O radiant peaks, that pierce the azure height,
Gemmed coronet wherein the splendours meet
Of heaven and earth entwined ! ye mighty walls
With vermeil or with glowing purple dyed,
Descending sheer to the green wave, and there
So mirrored, scarce is seen the line that parts
Hard rock from mimic semblance ! silver sands
Curving in lonely bays, from whence arise
The feathered forests, in whose dusky dells
Faint distant torrents roar, with misty spray
Nursing fantastic cordage of green growth !
What fragrant message from the flowery lawn
Bearest thou, gentle gale, of yonder isle,
Where palm and myrtle clothe the rocky marge !
If life and nature did not inly beat
With ever-changing pulse of keen desire,
Sure we our everlasting home might set
Within such paradise ; but vainly thus
We dream ; behold the tokens of man's toil !
The white-walled city, and the myriad masts
Fluttering with pennons ; and awakening men
Begin to stir, and send their hum afar ;
And dashing oars strike o'er the glittering sea.

E

Now were they parted who had comrades been
So many days, and each his several way
Wended.   But Dennell to the arid land
Far inland clomb, high raised on sun-scorched hills,
Where, deep engulfed in earth, a golden store
Lay for the labourer's delving hand to win.
For this should Dennell hold command and yield
Obedience ; for the cave was vast and deep,
And like an army were the men who toiled,
A dusky troop descending from white huts
Ere dawn, returning late at evening's close.
And in that service, while with hand and heart
Incessantly he laboured, on him came
The spirit of stern discipline, that is
The master weapon of all great design,
Like iron breaking hardest obstacles
That bar its way; his lip grew firm, that erst
Was flexible, in youth's soft openness ;
Keener his glance, erect his mien, his step
Swift, as a man that knows his work right well,
And must perform it ere the close of day ;
And brief his speech, and ever to the mark ;
So his esteem waxed higher, and the trust
Lent him by those who held the chief command.
But for the dream that was within his soul,
He told it not to any; no, albeit
It evermore shone round him, as the light
Of heaven's own day; devoid of which his strength
Had pined away, like plant in sunless cell ;
Yet told he none; the glory had been marred

By speech. But ever like a river flowed
Through him the thought of Helen : if he stood
In the dark mine, the winding passages,
Or by the huge revolving wheel that crushed
The stubborn ore, or on the lonely road
At eve among the palms, still 'twas the same ;
Still would that far-off glen and bygone hour
Send through his heart of hearts the springs of life,
As in some garden-nook which lies apart
From all the gay parterre nor ever feels
The gardener's tending hand, a secret stream
Will foster fern and flower.
                              Also at times
Gold-laden mules to Rio down the hills
With dusky guard he guided, well equipped,
Quick-eyed 'gainst sudden force or treacherous theft ;
So under hanging forests gained the shore
Of the long bay, and skirting, reached at length
The busy city ; sedulously there
Secured convoy to England of his store ;
Then in few leisure hours, while eve delayed,
Under the awning in some friendly house,
Or in thick leafy shade that screened the sun,
Held converse. Merchant, advocate, and priest,
Brazilian, English, men of various mind
He learnt to know, and heard the frequent strain
Of wrong that each had suffered, or the ills
From nature or from man's dark humours bred,
Or scheme political, or livelier jest,
Or some quaint fear, of superstition born,

That tames the strength of many, e'en the wise.
Conway he met, nor once alone ; and once
Farquhar, and Laura.   These were set to leave
The southern clime, and seek a cooler shore ;
The stalwart man, for all his strength of arm,
Had not availed to bring his labouring tribe
Into submission ; therefore his broad lands,
Teeming with weeds, sent forth no worthy fruit ;
His coffee trees, with long ungainly shoots,
Sprang high to heaven with berries scant and rare,
Best serving to some loitering rogue for shade
Who lay a-sleeping in the heat of noon.
His drying-floor, whereon the gathered crop
Strown evenly had dried apace, now lay
Gaping with cracks, in watery hollows sunk,
Walls ruining to dust, and gates unhinged,
Where beasts might enter, or the noxious snake
Lurk in the crannies, or the insect tribe
Unseemly live and die.   Therefore, at last
Despairing, he had sold his heritage,
Resigned to poorer but more genial life.
Yet "Courage !" with a cheery voice he cried ;
"Not I have erred, but Nature did me wrong ;
"She held me from the age when I was due,
"With my forefathers, men of mighty mould,
"To this degenerate day.   Your pardon, friends ;
"'Tis the unprosperous must praise themselves,
"For lack of gain.   A better day will come."
With Laura, then, who stood with brow serene,
He took departure : Dennell bade the twain

Kindly farewell, and wished their happiness,
And they to him in turn.

     But with Peranne,
Although a secret thread e'en now entwined
His lot with Dennell's, Dennell chanced to meet
But once in all his early years of toil.

Now as each circling year to June returned,
The chains of silence from the lovers fell ;
Soul flashed to soul across the ocean brine ;
Twice Dennell wrote, twice Helen made reply.
And this the tenor of his words at first :
" Thou sun of all my heart ! in whom afar
" I see hope's outline clear and heavenly ;
" How is each fibre of my nature wrought
"To bear its load by thought of thee, my Helen !
" Now do I feel that, as the electric spark,
" Most small and substanceless of things that are,
" Has power above the mightiest, such is Love ;
" For when I reckon up my enemies,
" I see three warriors ride atilt at me,
" And they are named Time, Space, and Circumstance ;
" With vizors closed they come ; against them I
"Stand armoured in thy love ; and lo ! their spears
" Fall, and are shivered in their idle grasp.
" Have I too boldly spoken ? if 'tis so,
" Helen, your lightest sign will bring me down
" Unto the common weary life of men.
" I do entreat you, tell me, love, if e'er
" My words offend. But now you needs must ask

" How I have prospered ; whether I discern
" Some way to fortune, such as may approve,
" E'en in your father's eyes, my worthiness.
" 'Tis a hard question.   There was one who left
" His office here, and found a vein of gold
" Among the mountains, and thereby attained
" To wealth ; but this for me were hazardous ;
" I can but wait and catch the fleeting chance.
" Yet ah ! I chide myself a thousand times
" For waste of sunnier seasons heretofore ;
" For hours in England lost, studies, and friends,
" Through whom much help had come. Companionship
" Is scanty here, although I bring no blame
" Against my comrades ; they are honest, good."
So did he write ; and added afterward
Much of the voyage, and of those he met,
Conway and Sylvia, Farquhar and Peranne ;
And of the mine, the darkness deep, the men
Who toiled therein, the tasks, and ordered rule.
Then ended thus : " My Helen, of yourself
" Tell me : forget not this ; and most of all,
" If e'er you have repented of the tie
" That binds us.   Also of your daily ways ;
" The friends you meet ; and if your father's health
" Be now restored ; and all his purposes.
" Say, if our glen lies sweetly desolate,
" As often in my dreams I picture it.
" Remember, unto me your hand's dear sign
" Is as one day of golden summertide
" Amidst a sad and tempest-stricken year ;
" It is my life."

So wrote he, and the lines
O'er ocean flew with speed to Helen's hand ;
Nor tarried then the maiden's answering word.
How she rejoiced, she wrote, to hear of him ;
And that he was with patience fortified,
She knew ; and she herself was strong in hope ;
She would not counsel ventures swift and rash ;
Though when due season offered, it were wise
To seek some change from that remote employ.
" Myself," she added " (you will smile to hear),
" Have changed the current of my life of late ;
" I am become my father's secretary ;
" I have experience of new men and things ;
" The tasks that once delighted me are now
" Fragments of memory ; think of me as grown
" Familiar with the turmoil of the world,
" Even as yourself.   No idler now am I ;
" Almost I failed, but 'twas through very zeal.
" For over-curious ever is my bent ;
" So would I weave conjecture of the sense
" Where to indite plain words was all my task ;
" And justly I was chidden ; but the hand
" Is cured of tripping by long use and care."
And having thus begun she added more,
Now of her lover's life, and now her own,
With tale or questioning, whate'er she deemed
Might serve to knit the severed threads anew,
As of some torn high-wrought embroidery ;
Nor laid the pen aside, but ended thus :
" My father sees this letter ere 'tis sealed.

" His health and strength grow daily ; so I trust.
" What more remains ?   You ask, if I repent.
" Think you, repentance shows itself in that
" Which I have written ?   Hark ! the stroke of one
" From the church tower booms out across the roofs
" That cover silent sleep : the noon of night
" Stole by so secretly, I knew it not ;
" Yet am I wakeful.   How doth this dark scene,
" That from my window stretches to those stars
" Which glance athwart the rack of driving clouds,
" Annihilate all distance ! for meseems
" Your message comes upon the blasts that drive
" Against our hills : O wild south-west, control
" This vehement fury ; let the voice I know
" Speak plainer to my sense !   Yes, Harry, now
" What you are saying, comes quite clear to me ;
" And I will tell it when we meet again."

Then Helen to her father ; " If you will,
" Read this ; for gladly I will show it you ;
" A letter.   'Tis for Harry Dennell's hand."
" Nay, keep it to yourself," he cried, and frowned ;
" Your writing is your pleasure, not my will."

Soon as the year had rounded once again,
Dennell to Helen wrote the second time ;
And after many loving words, " One thing,"
He added, " strengthens hope in me.   Long time
" I sought permission, granted now at length,
" To search by night the rifts within the cave ;

" Something, methinks, has been o'erlooked therein,
" Which with renewed experiment might show
" A quarry worth the winning ; but 'tis soon
" To ask if aught shall recompense my pains ;
" 'Tis but a week since I began to probe
" Each several track for clue or hint of ore.
" Meantime a doubt disturbs me ; this it is :
" Helen, I rule o'er slaves ; and is this well ?
" For some would say, it is a grievous sin ;
" If it be sin, it came not from my choice,
" But, as it seemed, from mere necessity.
" If sin it be not, blemish it must be
" Marring the honour of this land. And now
" The land itself is moved with questionings
" Concerning social justice ; and 'tis said
" That some with desperate zeal are filled, and plot
" For the state's overthrow ; such rumours vague
" Fly through the land, and are in part believed.
" Now, can I hold aloof, and say, these things
" Concern me not, being a stranger here ?
" You would not counsel thus. And yet what part
" Shall then be mine ? Is freedom's sacredness
" Stained by my office, by my every act ?
" Flatter me not, but tell the very truth."
And Helen in her answer, having writ
Of other matters, dear to him that read,
This added : " Well I know that nothing base
" Will stain your soul. If to your lot it came
" To see some dear affection torn and rent
" By law misnamed, you would not sanction it ;

" Rather returning to your native land
" Labour in shipyard, mine, or factory ;
" I'll ne'er abandon you in such a cause.
" But saving such event, I would not say
" That duty calls you to abandonment
" Of this your post.   Meantime consider this ;
" Lies there not much that may be ordered more
" For vantage of th' enslaved ? if it be so,
" Despise not gradual steps ; and foster hope
" In those beneath you of a brighter day ;
" Or at the least, with preparation train
" Their soul and intellect.   And speak to those
" In station like your own, as you may find
" Their minds respond, or fit to counsel you ;
" I would myself were wiser counsellor."
And Dennell did in all as she had said,
And grew in favour daily.

      But with zeal
Increasing, now he pierced those realms of night,
Seeking for some new vein.   While others slept,
He sought and e'en perused each angle, crack,
Hollow recess or passage ; till he knew
The bent of each fire-hardened rock as well
As his own home.   The solitary watch,
Who here and there was stationed in that maze,
Saw him full oft with lantern, axe, and rope,
Descending to the search.   Well served him then
The foot upon the Cumbrian mountains trained ;
How, down some subterranean precipice,
Oft would he let the lantern slowly glide,

While he along the narrow cramping ledge
Clomb slowly on 'mid silence vast and drear,
Save when some stone, dislodged and falling far,
Awoke a thousand echoes ! how, betrayed
By some false prop, that sunk beneath his tread,
Clung he with sudden grip of hand and arm
To jutting crag ! not without trembling then,
The peril past, could he sit down and think,
What easy unsought end his pains might find.
Anon the darkness-loving creatures strange,
Half beast, half bird, with flapping wings, disturbed
Out of their hollow haunts long time disused
By human footstep, at the unwonted ray
Would start in jostling, hurried, random flight ;
Or else, in lonely pool, the eyeless fish,
Shunning some strange o'erstreaming influence,
Wriggled away, and hid himself for fear.

And once or twice his prying eye had caught,
Sparkling aloft, the sudden gleam of gold,
Whither next day he sent the miner's axe
To quarry, not rewardless ; but a prize
Far greater shone at last.   It was the time
When southern summer draws the gathering rain,
When idly rolls the mist-encompassed sun
Defrauded of his due, who else would ride
Clear-flaming through his zenith's central height ;
The second year's third quarter lingered yet
Since Dennell touched Brazilian earth ; and now
The night drew near ; he hastened to his toil.

There was a chink upon a mighty cliff,
Unmarked before ; but so it chanced, that day,
When all the cave was as with glow-worms set,
One lantern's flash a moment lit it up ;
Alone he sought it.   Tying fast his rope
Unto a wooden shaft, the other end
Bound firmly round his waist, he clambered on ;
Entered ; of shallow depth it seemed ; but lo !
While with his axe he smote upon the rocks,
One stroke cut through ; a hollow gaped behind.
Now through the widened gap he clove his way ;
A glimmering grain flashed answer to his lamp,
Rightwards, and now to left, and now again
Back from the roof ; until not grains alone,
But a great vein of solid ore ran on
Zigzagging, roof to floor, and side to side,
Until the closing limit barred the way.
Breathless he cried : "O treasure house, what store
"In all thy chambers can compare with this ?
"And I have found it ! ah, were it but mine !
"Why for another's use must I still toil ?
"O ye that delve with axe and pierce with drill,
"It is but dirt ye bring to light of day,
"Now will I show you gold when morning dawns !"
So, to the wonder of his chiefs, next morn
He told his tale ; and trial gave reward
Better than expectation ; and much joy
Flowed to the hearts of those who held the mine
In ownership ; therefore with liberal mind
They gave a meet reward in moneyed store

To Dennell.   He, dividing, made three shares ;
One for his father's and his mother's use,
That they might know his love, and be consoled
In poverty's harsh straits ; the next, himself
As earnest of success retained ; the last
He sent to Helen's father, writing thus :
" The debt which through my father is my own,
" Seeing I am his debtor for myself
" By nature's law and long affection's due,
" Suffer me in slight measure to repay ;
" I pray you take it ; 'tis for duty's sake ;
" Acquaint me in due season only this,
" That no miscarriage keeps it from your hand."
With wonderment Dundas perused the words,
And shrewdly pondered in himself the while ;
" 'Tis a good youth ; and truly I am pleased ;
" An honest youth : but how to answer him ?
" There is the pinch ; for his audacious mood,
" I may depend on't, breathes a modest hint
" Of more than lies within the written phrase :
" His honesty, methinks, has eyes to see
" A mark beyond itself; for will he give
" The like to all his father's creditors ?
" A likely thing !   I see not yet the way
" To yield him up my Helen.   Shall I, then,
" Decline the gift ?—mere quixotry ! and rude,
" Savouring of quarrel-seeking and offence.
" Yet if I give that bare acknowledgment
" His letter asks, a danger lies therein
" Not less than by the overplus of thanks ;

" Helen would hear of it, and call me churl,
" And stir up angry words ; which must not be.
" Cautious, and brief, yet not discourteous,
" Were best reply."   And these the measured words
That crossed the deep, and came to Dennell's hand ;
" Sir, I acknowledge that which you have sent,
" And add my thanks to this acknowledgment,
" Thinking your father happy in his son."
And Dennell was well pleased with such reply,
And thought, " Now Helen surely will persuade
" Her father to more kindness ;" and the day
Was quickly nearing when his pen to her
Should trace the lines by new success inspired,
Breathing of hope and joy ; yea, that day dawned ;
It grew to noon ; but what befell thereon
Afterward, ere it sank again to eve,
Cannot be yet unfolded ; for the tale
Must backward run to other scenes and men.

O flower of joy, wilt thou
    Gladden the loving twain
With opening petals now ?
    Or shall the storm and rain
    Shatter the bud again ?

Though storm and hail and wind
    Beat on thy head, sweet flower,
In darkness thou shalt find
    The root that sends thee power
    Till love's reviving hour.

CANTO II.

PERANNE AND SYLVIA.

THE garden of our earth is sown with seed
Various, that in their growth aye intertwine
Each with the other; multiform their life,
Shape, colour, beauty, strength; yet evermore
Blending for peace or war they heavenward breathe,
And evermore the deep eternal root
Ministers succour to its like, until
In perfect order side by side conformed
They commune, life with life, and love with love :
So smiles the world, in fair alliance knit;
The pasture loves the feet of browsing kine;
The furrowy glebe the horse that toils and tills;
Wild rose and tangling honeysuckle mix
Their sweets, their hues; the forest's branching peers
Contend for high pre-eminence, yet ward
The winter's roaring blast from kindred heads;
So all beneath the sun's all-fostering ray
Join Nature's harmony, whose gathering tone
From age to age in ampler compass swells.

It has been said that Dennell with Peranne
Was joined by fortune afterward; e'en now
Their threads of life began to intertwine;
And therefore of Peranne the devious path

F

The song must trace.   He, standing on the shore
By Rio's bay—the voyage past, and words
Of light or tender parting interchanged
As each with each had mixed in friendly hours—
Felt through his weariness a seed of health;
Then from his many-coloured moods he grasped
Swift resolution; " Lo, I will take part
" In that stern struggle with our mother earth,
"Whence grow these earthly limbs, flesh, bone, and
        blood.
" Lo, I will find what message have the winds,
" When their swift coursers, sweeping o'er the sea,
" Make trial of the sailor's foot and arm,
" Who on the yard-arm furls the flapping sail;
"O ye whose hands with strain of ropes are hard,
" Horny, and brown, I'll be your fellow now;
" Your looks are life to me, and your rough tones
" Breathe music : thus my brain's perplexity
" And all the cares that hang around me still
" Shall die away.   What whisper in my heart
" Rises and checks me ?   Sylvia !   O fond thought,
" Cease thou awhile."   So saying, he embarked,
A sailor working for a sailor's wage,
On vessel bound for Chili and Peru ;
And clomb the mast, and met the breeze; his cheek
Gathered a browner hue ; then through the Straits
Of old Magellan named, in sudden storm
He showed a manful heart ; howbeit his hand
Lacked skill of seamanship.   But at the port
Of Valparaiso, by his gentleness

And knowledge of the language of those climes
He loosed a tangled strife between his mates
(Who from the shore of Massachusetts hailed)
And harbour officers, of Spanish pride ;
So did he win his comrades' favouring word.
But secret seeds were nursed in him the while ;
As an elastic cord, the more 'tis strained,
The stronger pulls, so, ever as he sailed,
Back flew his heart to Rio more and more ;
In visioned image that fair maiden stood,
He heard her voice, how dear and intimate !
So when the heavenly signs had circled once,
Amid the rainless countries earthquake-torn,
Where Lima's fanes are thronged, and on that shore
Where Chimborazo looks o'er Guayaquil,
He knew defeat.   And in that hour he met
(For so it chanced) a merchant company
For Paraguay with war's munition bound ;
Bidding his ocean-mates a swift farewell,
He joined himself to these, and through the clefts
Of snowy Andes won the central plain,
Mother of rivers ; safely thus he fared
Half-way across the mighty continent ;
But afterward he needs must journey on
With scantier guidance, and by devious ways,
For war was in the land ; then, overworn,
A sudden fever seized and brought him low
In poor rude hut of rough inhabitants ;
Yet he endured, and, perils past at length,
Borne gently down the river of the south

By boat and ship, and o'er the Atlantic wave,
He reached the bay of Rio, glad to win
Safe end of journeyings ; and thus he mused :
" Haven, my soul's sweet haven, let me lie
" Upon thy breast one peaceful hour, and think
" Of what thou art, and how thou shalt be writ
" In memory's pictured page some far-off day,
" When Time has drawn the curtain from life's scene,
" And things now dark are clear ; for now I stand
" At parting of two ways.   For say I quenched
" My soul's desire ; much safety then were mine ;
" In England, on the old familiar ground,
" A tranquil student I should pass the years,
" With intellectual keenness fashioning
" The thoughts of men; and men would praise the
        choice ;
"Success is surest where I know my strength.
" Then, sitting with my friends at wine some day,
" Talking of travels 'midst our leisured ease,
" I, too, might say, ' Truly my feet have trod
" ' The New World's soil; in Rio I have been,
" ' And seen the loveliest bay of earth ; ' and then
" Of form and colour I might speak, and trees
" And living things unknown to temperate climes ;—
" But this I should not dare to say or think,
" Save with a pang that pierced my heart like fire,
" ' Ah, and therein love's secret lay in bud,
" ' Waiting my touch to blossom, but I fled.'
" Come, heart of mine, be strong !   O love, thy voice
" Calls me from fair to fairer ; mysteries shine

" And spirits beckon onward, and I know
" The chain that binds me is the golden link
" Which fastens earth to heaven, and upward draws
" The spirits of all mortal men to share
" The heritage of gods (if to such name
" Immortal heroes answer), strength and light ;
" Therefore, vain bodings, hence ! my choice is fixed ;
" And yet betwixt me and that glory lies
" An interspace dark, doubtful ; thorny ways,
" And as it were a roaring flood, with marsh
" Encompassed round, scarce crossed by nimble feet :
" Let it be so.   Come, let me ponder well
" The ways of action.   Shall I seek the hand
" Of Sylvia with immediate urgent prayer ?
" That were too hasty.   I must wait awhile.
" 'Tis well ; for gladly would I learn to know
" The land where I must sojourn, more in full ;
" Which, so 'tis told me, raises now her head
" From ancient lassitude, the child of fear,
" And welcomes knowledge, freedom ; and I bear
" Letters from England that commend me well,
" To some in station here ; and I have means
" That will suffice me in this generous clime
" With frugal care.   Good hope is mine to thrive
" In this dear aim and all that thence may come,
" In after time, of honourable ends."
Thus he, by love impelled, devised his way.

And how had Sylvia fared ? and had she held
Memory of him that so remembered her ?

The open heart of youth had made her friend
To all upon the ship—from Farquhar now
Taking the lighter jest and compliment
With blithe repayment ; honest Hardiman
Amused her ear with lively college tales,
Or of the prairie life discoursed, and showed
His preparation.   Rarer were the times
Whereon she talked with Dennell ; for his air
Was grave ; and oft in silence he would lean
And backward look across the foaming waves ;
She understood him not, yet liked him too ;
And Laura Farquhar was the friend of all,
A kindly woman and a brave.   Howbeit,
'Twas on Peranne that Sylvia leant, and felt
In him the tenderer care ; for he would come
Ever obedient at her lightest call ;
Nor fruitless glanced his quick imaginings
Like flame of life upon her quickened soul,
But left a trace, a mark, that might be known
Hereafter.   But a woman, howso ruled
In intellect, is still superior found
O'er him that loves her ; so was Sylvia now
Queen o'er Peranne, and felt the joy of power ;
Nor till they parted on Brazilian shore
Knew she a sudden fear, lest he should pass
For ever from her sight and be of her
Mindless ; for now his venturous spirit urged
That second ocean-voyage ; so she turned
Crying, " And shall we never meet again ?
" Will not your feet bend hitherward once more ? "

Then he : " I will not seek my native land
" Ere I have crossed the threshold of your home,
" And told you all that I have seen and done."
So was she gladdened ; and on that new shore
A novel freedom for a while was hers.
A lady, quick of parts but narrow-souled,
Cousin to Conway, was by him designed
Guardian of Sylvia's youth ; Clara her name ;
Who should have been companion on the ship
To these her kin, and reached Brazil with them,
But was delayed, and later by a month
From England sailed, and tarried more at sea.
Therefore did Sylvia pass five happy weeks,
Because no guide or guard restrained her feet,
But over hill and dale she roamed, and talked
To whom she would ; her servant-maidens went
Ofttimes with her, dusky or fair of hue,
And taught her names and words ; the country speech
Grew more familiar to her ears ; and oft
She communed brokenly with fishermen
Upon the beach, or helped the aged crone
Whose withered fingers pieced the tattered net
Within the wattled hut of reeds and earth ;
Or with bright gifts allured the childish race,
Winning shy laughter from their shamefast eyes.
But Clara came, and freedom passed away,
Not by gradation slow and gentle lure,
But with a sudden curb ; and anger filled
The breast of Sylvia.   Now in weary days
Of formal duty did her mind return

To blither hours ; and as a traveller, spent
With desert wanderings all the sultry day,
Ever through vision of the inward eye
Beholds some green oasis, left at morn ;
So Sylvia thought upon Peranne, and e'en
With softer sense than when they sailed the deep
Together.   But the months wore on ; it seemed
He was unmindful of his word ; and she
Murmured, " The world is made throughout, I find,
" Of one same piece, and that of doleful hue."
You scarce would say she loved him, yet in truth
A hope was chilled.

              He sought her home at last ;
High o'er blue wave and glittering sand it stood,
With prospect far, and flowery-mantled trees
Spreading around ; but she was absent now.
Returning thence, he spied a dome of glass
Hard by the city ; men, but women more,
Passed in, or issued forth ; with curious mind
He entered.   Lo, a strange, fair, barbarous scene ;
For birds were fluttering, gorgeous-plumed, above
Through green embowering creepers, and it seemed
Those bright-winged prisoners must have yielded up
Gems of their beauty, such the dazzling glow
Of feathers ranged beneath, where maidens sit
Entwining many a spray that might adorn
Imperial pride ; and see, one rises now,
Laughing in chase, and wins her captive soon,
And, while he struggles, plucks a feather out ;
Released, he screaming flies, but not for long ;

Content, he trims with beak the ruffled plume.
Peranne turned round ; lo, Sylvia standing near,
With her the elder dame. But Sylvia's face
Flushed with surprise and pleasure, and she came
With cordial word and clasp of hand, and spoke
Her joy to see his hue of health returned.
He, with a smile that told of warmth within,
No less than hers, replied ; and Sylvia made
Her guardian cousin and her ocean friend
Each to the other known. But Clara looked
With doubtful favour on Peranne, and marked
How travel-soiled his raiment, and how worn ;
And over-cordial did she deem the phrase
And manner of their swift recognizance
On either side. She drew the maid apart ;
And afterward from Conway sought and learned
Peranne's estate, by fortune stinted much,
And something of strange humour in him bred,
Though keen his spirit ; therefore did she plant
Her will in stern discouragement, and chid
Conway as over-yielding. When Peranne
Essayed to visit Sylvia, Clara sat
Betwixt the youth and maiden, and by dint
Of ready speech and manner, held command
Of all discourse, and made it all her own ;
If e'er she suffered Sylvia's speech, it seemed
'Twas but the more to prove her in the end
A child, a weakling ; neither on Peranne
Spared she attack, but wondered why he stayed
In Rio ; glanced upon his need to work,

As humble in his means ; nor was amazed
For all his travel through wild lands, but gave
A slighting word of condescending praise.
And Sylvia scarce contrived a word to hint
A second visit.   When he came again,
Sylvia was absent, Clara sat alone,
Who froze him now with stern and scanty words
So, twice discomfited, he came no more.

But yet the vigilant lynx-eyed sentinel
Of this fair Hesperid was overwise,
And left the magic garden and the tree
Of golden apples by the western wave
Open to chance of unsurmised assault ;
For now Peranne began to linger oft
Among the boulders of the pebbly shore
At eve, in sight of Sylvia's home, that stood
High on a bluff beyond : and Sylvia chafed ;
Constraint itself, the clipping of her wings,
Had turned her thoughts upon Peranne the more ;
She wondered if he still were in the land,
And thought, if he had left without a sign,
'Twould be hardhearted.   Yet she deemed herself,
And seemed, all calm, like torrent on the verge
Of steep abysses, foamless ere it fall.
It chanced at length, one evening, left alone,
Down to the beach she wandered, and beheld
Peranne half lying, gazing o'er the sea.
He turned, he rose ; and when their hands had met,
She spoke the first ; and light the tone she feigned :

" Call you this keeping of your word ? " and he :
" Thrice have I sought you since the day I came
" Back from my wanderings." " It is well," she said ;
" Complete the promise that you made of yore,
" And tell me all that you have seen and done."
" You would be weary." " Nay, it is my wish ;
" Feign not excuse ; a traveller ever longs
" To tell his tale ; a listener here am I."
" Your care to know, fair maiden," he replied,
" Makes golden what were silver else, or bronze,
" When seen apart from that bright alchemy ; "
And thus beginning, he went on to tell
Of sailors, and the strange and hardy life,
Their minds of narrow wisdom full ; and then
The long lone nights, when reeled in storm and spray
The battered ship ; of sunnier days between ;
How from a boat they speared a mighty fish,
That tore them on with speed of hurricane,
Until it dashed its bulk upon the strand.
And Sylvia asked, " if ever he had met
" With savages ; " he thereunto replied :
" Hard by the land of ice and cloud and fire,
" Southernmost of all lands wherein men dwell,
" The dark-skinned native hailed us from his skiff
" In broken speech ; but ah ! what forms I saw—
" Half-human, naked, starving on the prey
" Won hardly from the ebbing ocean's marge ;
" Poor shattered fragments of our godlike race,
" As fading embers left to die away
" Far from the parent fire.   I turned, and lo !

" Nature majestic shone ; for glaciers streamed
" Into the clear green wave, and snowy peaks
" Pierced heaven's dome of azure crystalline,
" And shaggy woods through each long inlet ran ;
" Such glory and such sad dejection blend
" In one same sight !   But fiercer rovers swarmed
" Upon the central plain, where sick I lay,
" Stricken with fever in a poor rude hut ;
" I call to mind with what strange quietude
" I wondered if my blood would dye their spears.
" The gentler folk that nursed me, fled for fear ;
" Of Indian blood were they, but tamed of old
" By Jesuit fathers.''   While he spoke, the maid
Trembled for all his danger, though o'erpast ;
Not only tender did he seem, but brave ;
A thrill was in her voice as now she asked :
" Tell me, amid these perils, did you e'er
" Recur to all the learning, and the thoughts
" That strained your spirit once ? "   He made reply :
" He that is skilled can ne'er unlearn his skill
" Wholly.   And yet for many a month my hand
" Alone was active, and my brain inert.
" But when across the silent starlit wastes
" Eastward I fared, the ancient habit ruled ;
" For I had seen the Andes' mighty top
" Flame forth with glowing breath, that filled the sky
" And reddened earth ; methought this globe of ours
" Worked as with living instinct, and perchance
" Had some obscure and vital element
" That should be liberated and have course,

"When time is ripe, and strike the stars of heaven
" With sympathetic harmony, and join
" Their spheral choir and music heard of old
" By sages ; then the universe should breathe
" One symphony in endless growth divine."
" Ah !" Sylvia cried, "'tis yours to think and act
" As women cannot."   Now she paused ; in tone
A little bitter, added presently :
" It would be much if I could walk the shore
" In freedom."   He replied: " Is liberty
" So much in you restrained ? "   " What matters it ? "
The maiden answered ; " I was overquick,
" Saying the word ; the care is mine alone."
But then Peranne : " Nay, gladly I would know
" Your life is not unhappy."   "'Tis a road
" Girt in by high straight walls, and full of dust."
" It grieves me," he replied ; " I would my power
" Were as my will to serve you in your need !
" Only, to know that one has thought of you,
" May give you pleasure.   Since yon full-orbed moon
" Lay a thin crescent line upon the west,
" Too weak to claim her nightly rule in heaven,—
" Since then, and every eve, full twice seven eves
" That she hath grown in glory,—there is none
" Whereon she hath not seen my lonely feet
" Treading the pebbly beach, my thirsty ears
" Drinking the sound of waves or fierce or calm,
" Hoping to hear (but missing till this hour)
" Your voice, that mingled with the chiming waves
" So oft upon our voyage."

Sylvia sat
In pensive silence; for she seemed to see
How either she must yield her very soul
To him who spoke, to be commingled then
And in another's being blended more
Than any thought could sever, or must check
The word that he had uttered; hard the strain
In that brief moment of resolve and choice!
She raised her head, and lightly trembling spoke:
"You have been kind to think of me so much.
"But hark! that clock's shrill tongue bids me return
"Back to my home.   Suffer me one more word,
"And pardon it, for I have thought of you,
"As you of me.   It would be grief to me,
"If, lingering here, you lost some prize of worth
"In England.   Ah! I hear my father's voice;
"He calls me hence; farewell."   And he, "Farewell."
Clasping their hands, they parted on the shore;
But he past nightfall lingered by the wave.

Dreaming or waking
    Is it I lie?
The morn is breaking
    O'er earth and sky;

Where'er I look
    My love is seen,
In the rushing brook
    And meadows green;

From high cloud-towers
  She bends to me;
In fairest flowers
  Her lips I see;

The woods are ringing
  With her sweet voice;
What is she singing?
  " Rejoice, rejoice."

For joy to hear her
  My heart expands;
Now draws she nearer,
  I clasp her hands.

But what is this
  That clouds her eye?
What change of bliss,
  What grief is nigh?

Down falls the night
  With crashing thunder;
The whirlwind's flight
  Tears us asunder.

O sweet soft hand
  Unclasped from mine!
O sunless land
  Where all things pine!

The time was that when all Brazil in war
'Gainst Paraguay was fevered; when the stir
Of passion moved in divers ways, as each,
By chance of gain, or splendour of the fight,
Was inly urged; and e'en the muddy base
Of that high pyramid we name the State
Quivered through all the pressure on it piled
With throbs of life.   For Freedom's dawn was felt
Startling the air—that chief and first of good,
Which man within his inmost soul can feel
Though bound in chains; yet by the force thereof
Those chains will melt, when comes the ripened hour.
O seed too small for any eye to see
Where first it fell!   O plant by squalor oft
And desecration girt, and scorn of men !
O tree within whose glorious shade some day
All tribes of men shall rest, and life and truth
Eternal grow from root unconquerable !

Throughout the country went a sullen sound;
In alleys dark and dim, on open field
Or woody mountain, eye to eye expressed
The speechless token, ears drank in the thought
Unsyllabled but ringing in each tone,
Like to the cry of inarticulate things;
And last, the secret whispered word arose.
Then conclaves met in darkness; mean and poor
Gathered together, and the chain-worn slave :
And rulers heard thereof, but knew not where.

Now Sylvia's word had smote Peranne; "To her

"It would be grief if he should lose a prize
"In England, tarrying here." "If she," he thought,
"Bids me depart, it means not she is cold;
"Her bidding I must do; but first some word
"Of plain intent must show her spirit clear,
"Whether she will consent to ties of love."
He waited then, and looked for favouring times.
And in this interval he sought to know
The poorer city folk; and oft he went
Down to the port, and talked with those he saw,
Sailors, or workers at the iron ribs
Of ships that had been battered on the deep,
Or those that sold their wares upon the quay.
Now in the shipyard he had noted one,
Ferrara named, sallow, with raven hair
And hollow cheek, and strength was on his brow,
Yet something also sinister and fierce.
Who came one day and thus addressed Peranne;
" Sir, from your garb I thought you were of those
" The people's enemies, the cause of ill.
" But yesternight, when that poor woman fell,
" I saw you take her bundle on your back
" And help her home. I change to you, and think
" You are our friend, and ask you, Is it so?"
" Ay truly, so I hope," replied Peranne,
And after that, Ferrara and Peranne
Held converse often; and Ferrara told
The other of a meeting that should be
At dead of night, of such as fostered change
In great affairs, and bade him come thereto.

G

Peranne, consenting, went at eventide
Over the mountains, where a place remote
And lonely had been named.   With curious mind
He went; and yet an exaltation reigned
Within his soul as well, suspending fear;
He deemed that nought should unexplored remain
By one who would be pioneer and guide
To the world's future age.   Nor might he brood
So deeply but the sense of loveliness
In things around pierced through : the tropic night
Glowed with a thousand stars, and scents unknown
Were wafted by, and fireflies in the trees
Lit up their torches; ghostly mountain shapes
Seemed from afar to beckon.   So he gained
A crest, where sank the cliff; beneath was spread
A plain, not large, with woody walls engirt;
And men by hundreds stood or sat below.
Their humming voice, e'en as he looked, grew dumb.
Then, hastening down, he reached the level space.
Now on three stones that lay upon the sward
(Fallen from the heights) were three in vizors seen ;
Apparelled in great mantles, there they sat,
With torches three in front, that lit each fold
And seam upon their vesture, yet could none
Know form or face, so close were they enwrapped;
And at their feet, bareheaded, other three
Made deep obeisance, o'er whose neck the sword
Was stretched.   Howbeit a mask on every face
Repelled observant eyes; and loudly they
Made the profession that should consecrate

Eternal faith, that so henceforth their hand
Should move obedient to the holy cause,
Strike or forbear, at noon or dead of night,
'Mid multitudes or in the secret way,
As bidden of those appointed to command;
Their tongue in silence keep for evermore
Whate'er might harm the cause: thereto they swore
By the great splendour of the sun and moon,
By Aldebaran and Arcturus bright,
And by the planetary wanderers five;
And when they ended, other three in turn
Came with like words and lowly seeming mien;
And twenty-four were reckoned thus in full.
But then Ferrara, who had marked Peranne
E'en from the first, moved upward to a height
Above the plain; each feature was revealed;
With arms upraised and solemn look he spoke:

"Friends and companions! this our brotherhood
"Is consecrate, to wage eternal war
"Against the tyrants of mankind.   To-night,
"Ye who have stood, and made the truthful vow,
"Are the rich fruitful seed wherein the worth
"Of the far future ages hidden lies;
"Your hearts are firm in patience, and your hands
"Ready to act, your tongue will ne'er be false
"Or make betrayal of our deathless hope.
"Be joyful, then; ye bear a spell, as they
"Who move invisible through crowds; no bond
"So secret as your own in all mankind

" Is found ; from sightless distance ye shall judge
" Your haughty rulers, ay, and execute
" Your judgment ; therefore are ye terrible
" To those who ravage and insult the world.
" So much to you, the sworn and faithful ones.
" But now I speak a needful word to those
" Who share not yet in this our holy league.
" If any charge you, friends, with sluggishness,
" As tamely passive 'neath the rod, too dull
" To feel your pains—I will not credit it.
" O lift your eyes ! Behold, what plagues are these
" That fall upon you, and ye know not whence ?
" Famine, and fever in your noisome cots,
" Bereavements sharp and sudden, when the stroke
" Falls upon wife or child, who rot and die
" I' the dust untended, yet more dear to you
" Than theirs to wealthy, many-solaced men.
" Oh, is it not enough for them to live
" In palaces, where gardens of rich flowers
" Spread many an acre round, and lordly rooms
" Are hung with pictures for the eyes' delight,
" And for their taste unvalued dishes hold
" Delicate dainties ; where soft coverlets,
" Lest aught should bruise their fine white limbs, are
       " spread ;
" To shine in diamonds, and silk, and gold ;—
" Is't not enough, when they can look on you
" In dirty sunless dens, the spider's web
" Your chiefest ornament, and broken pots
" Your gaudy porcelain ? Were they but content

" With this comparison and pride of power,
" We could be patient.   But the chains they bring
" For chastening of your courage, prison cells,
" What tongue shall tell these woes ? what heart con-
    ceive ?
" Ay, some of you are slaves ; and some they drag
" Into the war.   What war ?   With Paraguay.
" And for what end ?   To crown our generals,
" Whose courage is thrice famous.   Better still ;
" It rids the country of ourselves, who are
" A cumbering rabble.   Garcia, you have lost
" A brother ; you two sons, Iachimo !
" And what the cause ?   Because the Paraguayan
" Has set his will against a despot rule.
" The wicked race ! or heroes shall we say ?
" O surely heroes !   Wherefore raise we not
" Voices and hands in aid of these, who fight
" Our common tyrant ?   Ye that hear me now,
" I proffer you two things ; of two things one,
" For both you cannot have.   On one side lies
" Obedience, ease, the life of sheep or kine,
" On whom men work their will.   The other side
" Is our companionship, so nobly knit,
" For freedom's sake, and right.   I would ye knew
" How many press therein !   And they shall sweep
" Your enemies from earth.   Choose, then, the good,
" And choose with speed, for time brooks no delay."

He ceased ; and cries applauding rose, the while
He from his height descended.   Slowly then

A hum, a motion in the crowd began ;
By twos and threes they walked; some cried, "Ay,
 burn
"With fire;" and others, "We must use our time ;"
Others, "How bravely, with what clarion voice
"Ferrara calls to act !"   But others used
A tongue unknown ; and most (Peranne did note)
Were clad in grey attire ; 'twere hard to say
What were their rank ; the poorest few alone
Wore coloured patches.   As he looked, a man
Out of the babblers' midst withdrew, and neared
The glen's steep side, then plunged amid the trees.
And while Peranne was wondering in himself,
"What secrecy is here ! I scarce could tell
"Hereafter one of these by face or garb,
"Saving Ferrara ;" hark ! a harsh, deep voice
Pealed from the mass, "A traitor—seize him, quick !"
And three pursuers clomb the woody cliff.
They, too, were hidden for a while ; at last
Emerging, with their captive reappeared :
Their faces half were shrouded ; his was bare,
And, by the torch illumined, pale as death.
Then rang the dreadful accents ; "Take him hence,
"And what is meet with traitors do with him !"
A throb of pain shot through Peranne ; "Alas !
"I am accomplice here to-day," he thought ;
Then sought Ferrara, but discerned him not.
With swift resolve he mounted on the rock,
Whereon Ferrara erst had stood ; the torch,
Dazzling his sight, hid all below ; his heart

Trembled, and yet with all his might he called :
" Listen ! "   A silence fell upon the groups
That nearer stood, and spreading like a wave
Reached to the furthest bound.   He spoke again ;
" Bethink you, how the way of bloody rule
" Is theirs, whom ye abhor !   I say no word
" Against your will—I loathe the chains, the pride
" Wherefrom ye suffer ; yet be merciful
" Yourselves, nor make your yoke like theirs, who crush
" The struggling lands with iron rod ! Th' oppressed,
" Shall he become oppressor ?   O take heed
" Lest blood be on your hands and turn and work
" Against you ; spare this man, and slay him not ! "
Scarcely at first Peranne was understood,
For in his speech the foreign accent rang ;
But soon the sense was plain, and murmurs swelled
Into a clamour ; and the nearest few
Rushed, and one struck him ; others jostling pressed,
Or brandished sticks before him ; two in masks,
Wearing the semblance of authority,
Advanced, and seized his arms, and led him down
Unto the dreaded presence.   But by this
Ferrara hurried up ; " Master," he cried,
" I had not thought that one, whom I myself
" Brought hither, would so far presume in speech
" Of daring folly.   Feeble is he yet ;
" He has no knowledge of ourselves, our plans,
" Our powers ; he neither can nor will betray ;
" I pledge myself, he will not seek our harm.
" But for the wretch Zamalca, were't not well

" To deal with somewhat less of rigorous haste ?
" Under surveillance he may tell us much
" That will advantage us ; no grain has he
" Of conscience or of courage, but will serve
" The nearest master, valuing his own skin
" More than the lives of all his friends.   If more
" You seek to know, in private you shall hear."
Then passed a consultation quick and brief ;
Which done, the hollow voice addressed Peranne ;
" Beware ! our arm is longer than you deem.
" Dismiss him hence."   With liberated step,
Not hasty, went Peranne his way apart
Under the silent heavens, until the dawn
Showed him his home amid the sleeping town.

———

Are hate and strife the way of life ?
    Strange paradox ! yet know this truth—
Through war's alarms and clash of arms
    Our earth resumes the fire of youth.

———

Though in Peranne ambition moved, and urged
To strange adventure, yet far more had love
Implanted wings of daring in his soul,
That bore him on in flight too swift to trace
The region round ; and universal trust
By that confiding light of Sylvia's eyes
Was kindled in him : therefore many a shape,
During those days, of murky guise impure

He passed unknowing ; wheresoe'er the cry
Of weakness rose, it drew his pitying soul ;
Poverty was a magnet to his eye ;
Far more he feared to lose one heavenly spark
Than by a thousand phantom fires beguiled
To roam through bog and fen the livelong night
Till the pale morn should rise.   But peril now
With sharp awakening sense reached his heart's core ;
As one that careless on a grassy bank
Had flung himself, and felt sharp thorns pierce through :
So when the sleep profound wherein he fell
After that night of spirit-vexing storm
Had left his eyes unsealed, at blazing noon
By shady lanes he wended to the port,
And found Ferrara pausing from his work ;
To whom he cried : " O what hast thou revealed ?
" What have I seen, when I had fain been blind ? "
Then spoke Ferrara, with a sidelong glance :
" Good sir, your pardon.   'Tis unfortunate
" That one vile inconsiderable thing
" Should make our worthy cause seem worse to you.
" The best things show not their best side at first.
" The youths that set their rude unseemly hands
" Upon you yesternight, our chief rebuked
" Their insolence most sternly : would that you
" Had stayed to hear it ! "   Then broke in Peranne :
" Not for my sake, Ferrara, am I grieved ;
" Rather for yours.   What hope you to advance
" By these dark ways, whose aim is but to check
" Old tyranny with new ? "   With quiet voice

Ferrara answered : " Call you that which men
" Embrace with willing souls, a tyranny ? "

" Name it howe'er you will," replied Peranne,
" It lacks the honest form of liberty."

Then said Ferrara, " Patience ; know you not
" That men must work with weapons that are meet
" And nigh for use ; not such perchance as they
" Would choose for pleasure ? Shall these hapless men,
" Slaves some in name, and all in very deed,
" Sit tamely down beneath th' oppressor's hand ?
" Is that your gospel ?   If you say, ' Not so ;
" With manly bosoms they should vindicate
" Their freedom freely ; ' 'tis impossible ;
" They cannot, if they dared.   But what they can,
" Is good for present purpose, when they strike
" Fear into breasts that held our prayers in scorn ;
" And crouching hearts shall feel reviving warmth.
" Is that not much ? Will you do more than this ?
" Yet more will come with time.   What better way
" Lies in your counsels, that shall aught avail ? "
Then answered him Peranne : " Tis true, that men,
" For some momentous end of happiness,
" May justly bind themselves with stern resolve,
" And with approving conscience execute
" Things that would else offend the sacred law
" Of human kinship ; but your edifice
" Is with cement of fear, and not of trust,
" Compact throughout. You say, that willingly

" Your comrades and your followers bind themselves :
" I grant it, for the present hour and day ;
" But the long lapse of weeks and months and years
" Will bring repentance, lure them gently back
" To the familiar ways, how mean soe'er,
" Grievous, and despicable ; rather this,
" Than 'twixt the millstones of this double sway,
" The open and the secret, to be crushed.
" I would not deprecate the swift sharp blow
" Of sudden action ; but far otherwise
" Your purpose holds.   You plant among mankind
" A strife, long, thorny, unappeasable ;
" All fruit of amity, that might be won
" From gentler foes in some relenting hour,
" You cast aside ; but wherefore say I more ?
" You go your way, I mine."
                              " That word is true,"
Returned Ferrara ; " in the rest you err.
" The fruit of amity ! 'tis a fine phrase.
" Were it not well, ere speaking of the fruit,
" You learnt where grows the tree ?   Hearken ; I'll tell.
" Love follows fear, as sequel and result ;
" Who fears not, loves not.   'Tis by blows of might,
" Not by entreaties, or by puling cries,
" That tyrants totter on their thrones of pride.
" Look you : the nice refinement of the rich
" Deems it indignity to touch the hand
" Of some poor drudge, horny, and coarse, and grimed,
" Whose abject mien betrays his impotence ;
" Call you that amity ? the severance stands

" Impassable, impregnable to prayer,
" Or soft reminders of our brotherhood
" In race or creed or mere humanity ;
" Seeing the rich man holds himself assoiled
" Of sin or fault against his ragged kin,
" If but he add not by fresh robbery
" To his time-consecrated plunderings.
" But let the poor seize favourable time,
" Prove himself master of the tools of fear,
" Wherewith to render blow for blow, and claim
" Some true equality of heritage,
" You'll see a different amity ! the rich
" Will reconsider, then, his old distastes,
" And find a something noble and divine
" In labour-hardened hands, when they have proved
" Their power against him."

                       " Ay, if this can be ;
" But 'twill not be, Ferrara.   Every point
" Favours your masters, saving one alone ;
" Which is, the pity in men's hearts for those
" Who suffer wrong ; resign not this, I say."

" I say, a scornful pity will be given
" To idle cries, unbacked by arms of strength."

" I love not vain lamenting," said Peranne ;
" But honest men will judge a worthy cause
" With truth at last ; and arms of strength will come
" With growing time.   You have my mind ; enough."

" Be it then so ; but let befall what will,"
Ferrara answered, " as our plans are set,
" So must they stand, for fruit or barrenness,
" For good or ill, for triumph or repulse :
" You come too late with counsel ; if your mind
" Goes not with ours, why then farewell ; but yet
" Remember, they who stand 'twixt foe and foe
" Are stricken oft the sorest stroke of all."

" Natheless your danger far surpasses mine.
" I would I liked your end ; but each man walks
" His several way, and bears his fate alone."

So from Ferrara did Peranne depart ;
Rare was their converse in the after days,
Till one momentous hour, whose aspect stern
Tarried for each, but with unequal doom.

INTERMEZZO.

Peranne and Dennell, one tempestuous day,
Met on the heights that overlooked the bay.
The one, escaped from tumult harsh and rude,
Lulled his wild heart in windswept solitude ;
Toilworn the other, yet of spirit free,
Led golden treasure toward the eastern sea.
The rain was past ; the valleys far and lone,
Headlands, and isles, in mellow glory shone.

Dennell.

All day o'er the mountains
  The stormcloud has lowered ;
The sky's teeming fountains
  Their burden have showered ;
How flashed the fierce levin !
  How smote us the wind !
But now in fair even
  Our mules we unbind.

Peranne.

Yet fiercer than lightning
  The flaming of strife
When Freedom, far brightening,
  Calls nations to life ;
O'er chains cleft asunder,
  O'er sceptre and throne,
The world's living thunder
  For ever rolls on.

Dennell.

Is war's mighty madness
  Thy watchword and star,
Thou prophet of gladness
  To nations afar ?
Will cannon or sabre
  Give freedom at last ?
In patience I labour
  Till strife be o'erpast.

PERANNE.

O sweetly hereafter,
  When labour is crowned,
Shall time flow with laughter
  And song breathe around ;
When brave hearts have ended
  The battle so sore,
And passions are blended
  In love evermore !

DENNELL.

Though clouds rolling faster
  Should darken again,
Yet Love is our master,
  The healer of pain.
With life's blossom laden
  He wingeth his flight ;
What youth and what maiden
  Shall share in his might ?

PERANNE.

With tears I pursue him ;
  For faintness I cried ;
Now nearer I view him,
  And Hope at his side.
Their radiance how tender !
  As sunbeams they smile,
That gild with soft splendour
  Yon foam-girdled isle !

BOTH.

All day from sky-fountains
   The rainflood has poured ;
All day on the mountains
   The torrents have roared.
Now scattered and riven
   The clouds flee away ;
Fair shine on us heaven
   At breaking of day !

Again upon the solitary shore
Peranne with Sylvia stood ; and now she led
Unto a creek where dwelt a fisher-wife
Beneath the toppling crag ; and Sylvia coaxed
By word and sign and smile the rugged dame
To lend a skiff. She set Peranne therein ;
But for the oars, she needs must handle them
Herself; she chid him, crying wilfully ;
" What profits it that every day at home
" I learn obedience, saving I may teach
" Others the lesson ? " in mock anger then
She knit her brows. He, smiling, thus replied ;
" Fair Sylvia, you are captain, I the crew ;
" So I obey ; but yet it were more meet
" The captain ruled with head, not worked with
     hands."
But she ; " It is my pleasure ; " and he gazed

Upon her dark and flashing eyes and lips
That hid their laughter, while she drew the skiff
Gently along.   The shore was left behind ;
The clear green wave in many a fathom showed
Coral, and seaweed streaming like the hair
Of ocean nymphs, and shells more dimly seen
Upon that ever-deepening palace floor,
And darting fishes strange.   But now Peranne
Wondered at Sylvia, and inquiring spoke ;
" Where learnt you, then, to ply the oar ? "   And she ;
" Knew you not that I lived beside the Thames,
" Until my father brought me o'er the sea
" To cheer his home ?   With cousins there I dwelt ;
" Among the waterlilies and the swans,
" Beneath the banks with purple loose-strife set
" And yellow vetch, I learnt to guide the boat
" In hot July ; I knew not then the heat
" Of tropic suns."
               They neared an islet, dense
With intertangled growth ; no foothold there,
Unless the axe should hew a level space ;
But they nor could nor willed to harm the spot,
Sacred to many a queenly palm that waved
A mute farewell as they receded thence ;
So by the sylvan torrent-riven shore,
Within a lone bay's jutting horns enclosed
They found a lawny isle ; the skiff's sharp bow
Grated upon the beach ; they leapt ashore.
Then Sylvia turned and spoke : " Is it a sin
" To cast away the cares of life awhile ?

                        H

" I have been like a caged and trembling dove ;
" You, the wild bird, have given me strength to dare
" Beyond the wonted bound ; and I have flown
" Unto the lone and lovely wilderness :
" Is this too bold a deed ? "   To her Peranne ;
" 'Twere base in me to say it, who am now
" By you consoled, restored : for I have been
" Much troubled, Sylvia, in my mind of late,
" By cares I may not tell, at least to-day ;
" With you I have a spell of rest and joy.
" Yet if you fear, we will return again."
Sylvia upon him looked inquiringly ;
Then cast her eyes around ; " See you," she said,
" Yon tallest palm upon our islet's verge ?
" Whose shadow now is cast upon the sward,
" Nor touches yet the sand, much less the sea ;
" Soon as the western sun descending throws
" That darkening image on the watery plain,
" Homeward the skiff shall bear us."
                                   Long the hour
That, dreamlike, held them happy, rapt away
From memories of the world.   And either woke
The echoes of the air with song : and first
Sylvia ; for she had asked if there might be
Nymphs of the wave and woodland ; and Peranne
Answered, invisibly to mortal eye
They still might live ; and Sylvia said she knew
A song a Grecian maiden sang of old
In such a place and hour ; and thus she sang :—

Ye that are ever
  Joyous and free,
Spirits of river,
  Forest, and lea ;

Ye that are listening,
  Fair ocean maids,
Deep in your glistening
  Emerald glades ;

Grant us your guerdon,
  Children of life !
Loosen our burden,
  Sorrow and strife !

So may we measure
  Sweetly the hour,
Here, where ye treasure
  Shell and sea-flower,

Or, on the verdurous
  Mosses reclined,
Sport with the amorous
  Wandering wind ;

(Ah, through the blossoms,
  Sisters, ye smile !
Blithely our bosoms
  Quicken the while ;)

Here, where your glancing
  Footsteps have played,
Follow we dancing
  Light in the shade.

Nature's free daughters,
  Scattering mirth
Through the lone waters
  O'er the green earth,

Say, when I seat me
  Weary at home,
Will ye not greet me
  Over the foam?

And afterward Peranne, just ere they left,
Breathed a soft parting to the scene and hour :—

O earth and sky and ocean,
  Like Paradise
  Ye greet our eyes
With living tender motion .

O hour of hours the rarest,
  What treasure bright
  With sunny light
For memory thou preparest !

Winging thy downward pinion,
  O swift and free,
  Hast thou the key
Of heaven's high dominion?

So sweet the smile thou wearest,
  Thy sister hours
  With wreathèd flowers
Shall crown thee queen and fairest.

"Look," Sylvia cried, "the shadow of the palm
"Touches the wave."   They left the strand; Peranne
Was rower now; the mainland and the creek
Were quickly won; along the stony beach
Homeward they walked in silence.   Then, in act
Of parting, Sylvia asked Peranne how long
He tarried in the western continent;
He answered, there were things that held him here,
But when they were resolved, he must depart.
"I may not ask," she said, "what things they are?"
Clasping his hands in hers, she spoke again;
"Forget not wholly in your English home
"The lonely maiden of the western wave."
"Never," he answered; and a fire was lit
Within their mutual eyes; he kissed her then;
No further word, but after pause they went
Each from the other.   Now the maiden closed
The garden gate, and vanished 'mid the trees;
A surge of soul rose sweeping through Peranne;
"It must be said!   'O Sylvia, be my wife!'"

" And she shall know each secret of my heart.
" What stayed the word that hovered on my lips
" This moment ?   But delay shall be no more."

E'en as he thonght the thought, did fate prepare
A blow he knew not ; ay, and smote him down,
While he was tranced in love's imaginings :
For unto Sylvia, as she crossed the lawn
In happy trouble, veiled with brow serene,
Clara, with brow of anger, from the porch
Issuing, exclaimed (the maid astonished stood) ;
" O shameless ! what beheld I with these eyes ?
" What hast thou suffered him to do to thee ?
" Ay, him : thou know'st him not, but false is he :
" A deep-dyed villain ; e'en to name to you
" The places he frequents, or what vile folk
" Are his familiars, would in me be shame ;
" Of wantonness and crime his life is full ;
" I tell you, I have proof unshakable."
And Sylvia heard, and in the midst of pain
That through her ears found passage to her soul,
Remained incredulous ; at last, with voice
Low but distinct she spoke ; " You are mista'en."
And in that moment on her memory flashed
The word Peranne had spoken of the cares
That troubled him of late.   But Clara pressed
With more insistence, and required to know
What Sylvia would not tell ; and made demand
That she should promise never with Peranne
Again to commune.   Now did Sylvia seem

Stirred and transformed ; in anger she repelled
The charge that dared not clothe itself in words ;
Out of demure obedient maidenhood
She was aroused to passion new and strange.
But Conway came ; the father's added weight
Thrown in the scale against the daughter's will,
At last prevailed ; she promised as he bade ;
Then weeping fled, and sank upon her couch,
Crying, " Can all be false ? if all indeed,
" Peranne is guiltless ; but I fear he hides
" Some grievous secret trouble ; wherefore hide,
" Save from the conscience of a wrongful act ? "
Weary, she fell asleep at dead of night ;
Nor woke until the lengthening shadows turned
Eastward, and from his zenith's height the sun
An hour had stooped toward his western goal.

And after that Peranne, though seeking, missed
Her whom he loved, and knew not why he missed.
Now did he fear, yet knew not cause of fear.
One day he saw her ; none was near ; he ran
(For she had seen him not, yet half he thought
That she was bent on hurrying from the place),
" Sylvia," he cried ; she heard and stayed her step ;
Then turned with pale and troubled face, and spoke ;
" I cannot stay ; oh, leave me ! ask me not,
" Question not wherefore."   But the word was now
Hovering upon his lips, and must take flight ;
" Sylvia, I love you ; were it the last word
" That ever from my mouth on earth should fall,

" It is the truth."   But she, with hand outstretched,
Grasped at a fence (or else had surely fallen) ;
And he did note that she declined the hand
Which, to support her, he was fain to lend.
At last, with look beyond all speech, she cried ;
" They say you are a villain ; I did not,
" Nor will, believe it; yet perhaps——   Alas,
" What know I ? something you have kept from me.
" What says your conscience ? Nay, defend yourself,
" If you are true and good."   As if afraid
Of her own words, she fled.   He, desolate,
Stood there, how long ? the hours count not such time.

———————

The soul's deep visions touch with joy or pain ;
    But whether this or that, one scarce can know
In doubtfulness of hope ; if hope be vain,
    The flattering image may be direst woe.

———————

Hardiman, journeying from the southern plains,
Tarried in Rio for a little space ;
And wondering met, whom far away he deemed,
Peranne.   Well pleased they saw each other there ;
In mutual converse passed the day from noon ;
Hardiman spoke his gladness that his friend
Had won back health ; but noted in his talk
A jarring touch, a cynic bitterness,
As of some grief corroding secretly ;

Then asked the cause.   With heavy sigh Peranne ;
" The pit of darkness is dug deep for me,
" And I therein engulfed a helpless prey."
Thereto the other, more amazed, replied ;
" This is mere sickness ; your old malady
" Has ta'en new form.   Come hence ; the English shore .
" Awaits you ; shake the noisome dusts away
" That round this hot and alien region cling ;
" Seek out your natural comrades, and the air
" That you were born in ; then these mists will fly
" That here encompass you.   O think, your prime
" Of youth is wasting, perishing away !
" You, once among the ablest, now will rust
" Like a sharp-tempered sword thrown in the mire,
" If here you dream unroused."
                                Peranne was stung
By such kind speech ; " O Hardiman," he cried,
" I owe you thanks ! 'tis true that bitterness
" O'erflowed in me too much, and mere despair
" Is error ; yet I must defend the choice,
" How strange soe'er it be, that holds me here.
" Of men's esteem I am not careless grown ;
" 'Tis not so easy for the mind to doff
" Her old ambitions, that were bred in her
" By seed of fire, and nursed with yearlong toil ;
" But there is that within us, to whose power
" Ambition yields.   Your memory, Hardiman,
" Will not have lost the trace of those who sailed
" Our fellow-voyagers from English shore ;
" Of these was Sylvia Conway one ; and she—

"What must I say? I say not more than truth;
"She ne'er repelled me, or by word or look,
"Save for one cause; a lie has made me seem
"A villain in her sight, and profligate.
"Howbeit her heart acquits me, as I deem."
Then Hardiman put question of the whole,
And having learnt the matter, point by point,
Pitied his friend, but deemed he had too much
Followed the impulse of an eager mind.
Then said Peranne, "If Conway would believe
"The very truth, I would to-morrow sail
"For England. I have sought him, and indeed
"Moved him, I think; but he distrusts me still.
"How should I e'er seem honest in the eyes
"Of Sylvia, if I sailed for England now?
"No, whatsoever height were won by me,
"This memory would abide, and taint me still.
"Therefore I stay in Rio. Hardiman,
"You yet shall hear of me in better guise."

"Courage," said Hardiman; "indeed I trust
"To see you prosperous; and perpend the chance
"Of gains and losses: 'tis not worth your while,
"E'en to be righted in a maiden's eyes,
"To waste a life."
                    To other themes they turned.
Then Hardiman made offer, and Peranne
Feared not acceptance, of such help in gold
As should surround his days with cheerier light.
Till midnight hours they talked, then bade farewell.

Next day, at chime of noon, the wind-filled sail
Bore Hardiman from that Brazilian bay
O'er the Atlantic toward the elder world.
But ere he left, with care he sought and found
Conway, and in his converse mingled words
(Chance-strown as they might seem) that should commend
    Peranne, as one among the voyagers
That had accompanied their outward sail;
Whom Hardiman had likewise earlier known;
Guileless, adventurous, keen for novelty;
That Conway so should better understand
The man's true nature; gently then he passed
To speak of others, lest design should show;
And Conway truly by some grains of doubt,
Of softening purpose toward Peranne, was touched;
Yet not in act he changed.   For change is bred
In secret silence all insensibly;
True offspring ne'er was ripened in an hour.

Meantime Ferrara and his comrade band
Were urged to sudden haste; for fear had grown
Of lurking treachery, unsurmised before.
Therefore they set their strength for instant act;
That so through fiery ruin they might raise
Armies for overthrow of rule and law.

———

An angel dream, from heavenly brightness flown,

Came to Peranne when Hardiman had gone,
And cheered his sleep ; at morn he wrote it down :—

My love came to me in the night,
   She came in vision bitter-sweet ;
Gently she glided up to me,
   And knelt her down before my feet.

Upon my hands she laid her own,
   Soft as the falling snowflakes are ;
Her eyes they were not bent on mine,
   But rested on the heavens afar.

Her face to mine it was so near,
   That with my lips I kissed her cheek ;
With trembling lips I kissed her twice,
   Three times I kissed, but dared not speak.

I dared not speak, for so had flashed
   The fire that burned my very heart ;
Alas, my love ! alas, dear love !
   And didst thou know and yet depart ?

But if she loved me or if no,
   I knew not ; never word she said ;
She cast on me a pitying look,
   And with the breaking daylight fled.

CANTO III.

THE CONFLAGRATION.

But Sylvia rested not ; her cheek 'gan pine ;
For ever pondered she on things of doubt ;
Whether Peranne were evil-souled indeed ;
Whether herself were cowardly and false ;
Whether it stood required in duty's bond
She should unclasp the burden from her heart,
That once was not a burden, but a joy.
And looking up to heaven she sighed to see
Some flash of ireful power that should dissolve
The dull-drawn languor of this niggard scene,
Be it through lightning, earthquake, ruin, death ;
But ghostly visitant was none ; the air
With sickly quiet wrapped her fevered sense.
And thus her father, whom not now, as erst,
She met with candid open lineaments,
But with constraint, or fickle levity,
Or feebly listless, spoke in sudden mood :
" Sylvia, I am a careless gardener ;
" And you, my flower, are stinted of the wave
" That should refresh you in the summer heat.
" There is a wise physician on the hills,
" Who under shadowing boughs has set his home ;

" The forest spreads around ; and many there,
" Guests for a season, win the hue of health.
" Abiding in such resting-place your cheek
" Will blossom newly.   Thither let us go."
And so it was ; and Sylvia there abode
Three months, and strength revived in heart and limb
(Whate'er her secret soul's imaginings) ;
And twice her father came to visit her ;
But the third time she made request this wise :
" Father, I learn that one, our comrade erst
" Upon the ship that bore us from our home,
" Whom twice since then we met upon the shore,
" Lives scarce the journey of a day from hence.
" 'Tis Henry Dennell ; for the mine of gold,
" Wherein he is an officer, is set
" But little way beyond our forest's bound.
" Right gladly would I see him once again.
" His was a cordial face ; and travel lends
" New sights, new sounds, new breath of earth and sky.
" Take me, I pray ; old things have wearied me."
And readily her father lent his ear.
So in the early starlight, ere the dawn
Flushed through the heavens, from the friendly roof
They took departure, riding down the steep
On back of mules that feared not crag nor stone,
Surefooted in the darkness ; and anon
The o'erarching forest glimmered green above,
Or parting in long vistas showed afar
The billowy ridges surging endlessly
In misty light ; and now the treeless tract,

Barren, yet rich with buried ore, was won.
And Dennell from his dwelling came, and gave
Surprised but cordial welcome; and they marked
The token of success in mien and look;
But he in Sylvia noted somewhat strange,
The glance, the motion, full of feverish fire;
And then he asked them to come in and rest,
For that the heat was growing still in heaven.
He set before them cooling drinks, and fruit
Of tropic growth, fresh from the garden culled;
And told of all his labour in the mine.
And Sylvia hearing cried, " How fresh and cool
" The darksome depth must be, this glowing day!
" Father, I fain would see it.   Let us go.
" You, sir, will guide us?   Nay, refuse me not!"
For Conway checked her eager speech with fear.
" Nay, child, your brain will reel, your limbs will fail."
But Sylvia pressed the more: " O suffer me!"
And urging thus, she won her will at last.
(But Dennell thought, " To-day I should have writ
" To Helen; it must wait to-morrow's dawn.")
So to the hollow opening, where the gulf
Sunk downward from the bright warm day, they went.
There was a slanting shaft that mightily
Stretched in the downward darkness.   Either side
One ladder served for feet of goers-down,
And one for those that sought the blithesome air.
But twice a thousand steps must he descend,
Whoso would reach the glimmering lamps below;
And twice a thousand upward, who beholds

I

From the ore's couch the mellow mists of heaven.
In fear they shrank; then spied an easier road.
Over the ladders sloped a wooden way,
Fast-fixed with nail and rivet in the walls
Of that vast cavern; thence a vessel hung
Of iron, massy, held with massy chains;
Therein they stepped, and it began to glide.
See, as it moves, how by the flaring torch
The silent rocky chambers stand revealed
Each for a moment, then in darkness drowned,
Deep-sunken vistas!　See the stalwart girth
Of forest trees, torn from their sylvan homes,
Where many a day they breathed the summer air,
Fanned by the winds, beside the bubbling brooks,
In leafy glory; now in gloom condemned
To prop the sunless mansions, never more
To bud and sprout, and feel the circling sap,
But lifeless to subserve another's use,
Reft of their being, bound in black constraint,
Multitudes, multitudes! like ghosts that dwell
Beside the dreary Acherontian wave;
Some at the right hand, some beneath the feet,
Some on the left, in shallow niches some,
And some in rows that faded in the night.
Then Conway cried, " How if the fire should seize
"This ancient grove immense, that holds secure
"The monstrous gulf?" But Dennell smiled, "'Tis safe;
" Compact, hard-grained the wood, and moist the air."
Down, down they fathomed the unending road
Faster and faster, till the giddying whirl

Perplexed the brain, and made them scarce to know
Whether in truth their flight were up or down,
Or rather it appeared the opposite
Of that which was, as if the central earth
Had changed her being, and repelled her brood
Into the void dark space.   Slackened their speed
At length ; and lights, that erst as tiny stars
Had moved in that abysmal night beneath,
Now into torches flamed ; the hammer's clink
Ceaseless re-echoed on the hollow walls ;
And cries were heard, and chants monotonous
In weird refrain, and shovelling of huge stones ;
And drip of pattering waters on the pool
That lowest lay ; thereat they touched the floor.
Then do they see the length, this way and that,
Through vaulting arches in the vast obscure,
Immeasurable as the height above ;
Cathedral-like it seemed, but not as those
Where at bright morn and tender eve the ray
Through ruby-purple windows softer falls,
Tinging with alien hues the white-robed choir,
Whose hymn soars up along the traceried roof
And listening nave to heaven.   Far other here
The ministry was set ; swarthy and stark,
The brawny shapes of Titans in fierce toil,
Suspended in the dusk aërial crags,
Or heaving, hammering, in each long recess,
Their swelling muscles lit with smoky glare ;
So do they stir the stubborn heart of earth
For treasures that shall never be their own ;

Poor hands, poor souls, with labour hard and dull !
Rewardless of all beauty; not for them
Joy of wide heaven, or freshly blowing winds,
Nor the high will, the far unfolding hope,
That sheds o'er pangs of pain clear-visioned peace ;
Nor can they e'en rejoice that by their hands
These halls of night were delved.   Like ants they work
Their little lives in darkness, and then die,
Unconscious as the waves that rise and fall,
Each after each, in the mid-deep unseen.

O thou, that like a sorrowing Niobe,
Watchest thy children ! thou deep presence, nurse
Of life, warm love, and fount of love through all !
What recompense for sad fidelity
Bearest thou in thy bosom ?   What far clime
Shall foster fruit in these, whose seed is shed
Here in the wilderness of rugged dearth ?

Now while they stood in wonder at the vast
Concave of darkness pierced with many a torch,
Behold ! a runner from the furthest bound
Approaching cried, " A fire in Poncha's lode,
" Sir, asks your presence straight ; an hour or more
" The spark has held his mastery of the wood."
" Why told ye me not sooner ? " Dennell cried.
" Sir, 'tis but just discovered ; for the lode
" Lies backward, and the nearest workers left
" Their post at noon, and are returned but now."
To Conway and to Sylvia, Dennell turned :

" Danger is none, my friends ; yet best it were
" You sought the upper ground.   This man will see
" Your safety sure."   He spoke, and pulled the wire
That to the upper air the bidding gave
For swift ascent ; already had the three
Stationed themselves within the iron car.
They vanished upwards ; he a whistle took
Suspended from his belt, and shrilly blew :
The workers stayed.   " Away to Poncha's lode ! "
He cried, and speeded o'er the uneven floor.
Then might you see the workers high aloft
Unwind the chain that bound them, and adown
With glimmering torches glide the steep crags o'er :
So up the ladders and through labyrinths
Of many a winding way and gallery
They went, until they reached the place they sought.
There stood a giant pillar, whose great side
Of solid oak compact, the fierce flame now
Was hollowing to a crescent ; roaring blasts
Sweeping again and yet again made more
The fire by which themselves engendered were ;
Dense, eddying smoke, half black, half lurid red
O'erhung.   No idlesse there, but to and fro
Men hurried breathless, or with buckets poised
Flung on the burning pile the watery flood ;
Or laid the leathern channels, joint by joint,
Where through the quenching element might flow.
But Dennell's eye scanned the fire's upward range.
Then one that followed spoke : " 'Tis lessening now."
" God grant it so ! " said Dennell ; " yet, yet mark

" The growing smoke above."   Then, with a voice
That rang both loud and clear and far, he called :
" Why loose ye not the cistern stored above ? "
And one made answer : " This is some one's deed ;
" The cistern's store was tapped before we came."
And Dennell hearing this recoiled, and gasped
Like to a man stabbed by a sudden blow,
Or as one 'ware of evil standing near ;
Yet not for long ; with swift recovery,
" Then have ye sent," he cried, " to watch the mine,
" And guard each several part ? "   " Ay, sir, 'tis done."
" And to the upper air ? "   " Not yet ; is't need ? "
" Ferguson, lose no moment !   Haste aloft
" With all your men, and ready make the sluice
" To pour down each main shaft.   Hammick, be 't yours
" To cut away the timber round the fire.—
" Damnable villain !—Quick, my men—quick ! quick !
" Who speeds to-day, it shall not be forgot ! "
So they with toil, and sweat, and pain, and heat,
Strove in that worse than darkness to o'ercome
The fiery essence, that would fain destroy
All works of man, and bring rude chaos back.

And where was Conway, where was Sylvia, now ?
Ah, still in that deep cavern dark engulfed.
For after they had ta'en their upward flight,
A little while and slower it became,
As if some hindrance pressed ; at last it ceased.
O what a blackness, what a silence then !
Expectance grew, and wonder, and now fear ;

" What holds us here ? " said Conway ; then the guide,
" I'll to the top.   Sit, stir not from your place."
So were they left ; and neither spoke, but each,
Enwrapped in thought unshared by th' other, sat.
For Conway thought," What arrant fool was I,
" At bidding of my wild-brained daughter here,
" To rush on this mad scheme ?   She deems the whole
" A jest ; nor profits it to speak of fear."
But Sylvia's fevered pulses and quick moods
And agitations long in silence nursed
Through days and weeks, in the clear light above,
Took a strange calmness in that strange dark place ;
For outward ill, to heart and nerve o'erwrought
By spiritual pain intangible,
Is oftentimes relief ; and so when time
Grew lengthening on, still quietly she spoke :
" 'Tis certain, father, there is danger here."
But Conway rose, and grasped the iron chain
That held the car, and bent his listening ear ;
" Daughter, I hear a step."   And now the guide
Descending showed a lantern.   " Haste," he said,
" A little way, not far, up these rough steps ;
" Another shaft we needs must try.   A nail
" (Through malice or by chance, we know not yet)
" Had caught and torn the rope that drew us up,
" Which when we sought, we could not safely loose.
" Here, lady, put your foot upon the round ;
" Fear not ; my foot supports you ; this the way."
So to the second gulf precipitous
Laboriously by arched and narrow paths

They went, and by the lantern's light beheld
The vehicle prepared ; when Sylvia's eyes
Glanced upward and caught thence an ominous sight—
A little flame, a serpent's tongue, flashed out
From the opposing wall, and died again.
"Alas !" she cried, "this is no way for us ;"
And while the other two in wonder gazed
Upon her, lo ! no more a serpent's tongue,
But as a great leviathan's breath of fire
Darted the lurid column from a coil
Of thick involving smoke, the master now
Apparent of that dusky toilwon realm.
Conway in fear seized Sylvia's arm, and cried,
"Come, daughter, stay not ; for we needs must now
"Surmount the ladder, howso hard it be ;
"Come quick ! What, are you mad?" For Sylvia clung
Unto a stone that hung above the abyss,
And gazed on every corner that was lit,
How terribly ! yet beautiful to see ;
For a great beam had fallen, and in the depth
Burnt still, and lightened up the long arcades ;
The massy face of stone, half wall, half roof,
Hung sloping hugely (never seen before
As now, in that strange glare, by mortal eye).
Then vaporous blackness grew again o'erhead.
But Sylvia cried, "A terror seizes me !
"Are they whom we beheld an hour ago
"Within yon burning pyre ; or where are they ?
"Oh, ere we go, bethink you, can aught reach
"Their living forms and help them to the light?"

E'en as she spoke, a murmur of dull sound
Seemed from the depth to rise, they knew not where;
Nor long, when lo! out of the smoking vent
Of a strait passage-way that lay beneath
Came one at running speed; black was his face,
And black and torn his garb, yet plain to view
Was Dennell.   When he first upturned his face,
He saw the flame, and made so loud a cry
That all the walls re-echoed; then a crowd
From each dim gallery rising gathered round,
As from their waxen cells the swarming bees.
They stood amazed, astonished; "Who," he said,
"Who thought of this?   The fire has mastered us."
A second time he upward glanced, and saw
Conway and Sylvia; leaping then he sprang
And set his foot where space for foot seemed none,
And stood beside them.   "Ah, how came you here?"
"The rope betrayed us."   "Haste, you must away!
"Hammick, command the rest while I am gone.
"Lady, I pray you come;" for Sylvia glanced
Wildly.   "Will all be safe?"   "Ay, if you go."
She said no other word, but led the way
So truly, Dennell marvelled; then they reached
The shaft, where stretched the ladders in the dark.
And Conway clomb the first, and Sylvia next,
Dennell the last.   And now they neared the top,
Already gleamed the sunlight on the side,
When Sylvia cried, "I faint!" and backward fell.
Dennell was ready, and his arm was strong;
He held her up and bore her to the light.

Further he lingered not, but laid her down ;
Conway was nigh, and need was great below.

But Sylvia opened from that swoon her eyes.
Her father's arm was under her ; he spoke :
" Say, are you hurt ? "   She thrust her faintness back,
And lightly trembling stood upon her feet :
" Nay, I am well.   My father, it is strange
" That this has happened, and in such an hour.
" Long have I looked for something like to this."
Conway perplexed and anxious heard the speech.
" Sylvia, you have been overwrought ; the scene,
" The fear, the danger, colours still your thought."
" Nay, but I did not fear.   Oh yes, indeed,
" I feared, I fear, for those that are below !
" They succoured me ; O who shall succour them ?
" My petty life is naught in such an hour."
Conway replied, " We have no help to give
" In this sharp stress.   Come back to Dennell's house ;
" Rest there ; and we will wait until the end."
He led her gently thitherward ; but she :
" I will not enter ; let us stay without."
And Conway mused in troubled thought, but yet
Knew not what word to say, so calm and still
She on a sudden seemed.   Once more she spoke :
" Father, 'tis true that you were right herein ;
" I was too weak for such an enterprise."

So before Dennell's house they sat and watched
How the four shafts, in even order ranged,

Sent up four smoking columns to the sky,
That denser grew each hour; and now a sight
Of terror and of pity met their view:
From the black gulf of night is borne of twain
A man sore-stricken; hue and hair and lips
Revealed the Afric blood, but all his limbs
Below the thigh were shrivelled, scorched with fire;
Yea, and all crushed and battered from their shape,
Which, from the fashion of his chest and arms,
Must needs have been in comely strength adorned;
Save for a groan, you would have deemed him dead.
And Sylvia shuddering turned her eyes away;
But to her father's prayer that she would rest
Yielded no whit: " I too will see the end."
It was the hour of eve, but alien far
From rest and peace; and now a crowning woe
Was piled upon the sum of terrors past;
For lo ! the second opening of the abyss
(Wherein their safe ascent had erst been foiled
By sudden darting of impetuous flame),
Like a volcano from its fiery gorge,
Belched a bright column; and a gust of wind
Bore sparks toward a heap of logs that lay
Against the huts; and Conway without word
Rushed to remove that seed of fatal ill.
But all too late; already were the walls
Caught by the blazing element, that rose
For swift destruction of the workers' homes.
And none were near, so Conway called aloud—
Three times he called, as if to split the earth

And reach the depth below ; yet Sylvia pierced
Further with her shrill cry, and waved her arms
Like frantic Pythoness ; but most the fire
Screamed his own birth, like eaglet from the nest
(For first in low recess it had been hid),
And licked the roof with lambent tongue, and thence
Careered in triumph, as defiantly
Rejoicing to defeat the darkening night,
And shame the enfeebled stars with conquering glare.
And from the depth and from the distance now
Were gathered many ; and they brought for aid
The blasting powder, and laid waste a part,
So to confine the ruin in strait bounds,
Wherein they prospered ; and the midnight hour
Gave back the eternal lights of tranquil heaven,
Gave to the miners half their homes secure,
The other half in smouldering ashes smoked.
Meantime that subterranean conflict raged
More sternly far; but when the crashing boom
Of thundering stones from all the vaulting roof
Of the mine's lurid regions token gave,
That unto man the victory should not be
'Gainst those awakened Titans, slumbering erst
Within earth's entrails, now for slaughter armed,
Then was the order issued to ascend ;
And up the ladders swarmed the vanquished brave,
And spread upon the plain ; you scarce could tell
Afric, Brazilian, English, each from each,
In that half-naked, torn, begrimed array ;
And many wounded were upborne by hands

Of comrades seeking succour, for they saw
Then first their ruined homes, and knew not where
Refuge should be.   But one that seemed to hold
Authority by gesture, look, and voice,
Pointed to Dennell's house, that nearest lay ;
So whosoe'er had hurt of maiming stone,
Or scathing burn, or choking poisonous wind,
Was carried thitherward.   But Conway saw
With sad dispiritment of boding fear
Such movement ; for he thought, " They surely deem
" Our friend has need of earthly home no more."
Therefore with Sylvia he withdrew, and spoke
To him who held command : " I pray you, sir,
" Tell me of Henry Dennell, if you know.
" He is my friend ; his guest was I to-day.
" Lives he as yet unharmed ? or has some hurt
" O'erta'en him in this dire calamity ? "
Thereto the other in sad tone replied :
" You touch upon our greatest loss to-day.
" Just ere we gave the order to ascend,
" Dennell was seen hewing with mighty blows
" Some wooden piles that joined the burning tract
" To this last shaft that was untouched by fire.
" So did he hope to save it ; but the flame
" Crept stealthily by narrow grooves above
" And winding cracks ; he heard, he saw it not,
" E'en when it caught with red devouring tongue
" The timber scarce ten feet from where he stood
" Smiting so lustily.   But one sprang down
" To warn him of the peril, yet too late,

" A negro ; for that instant blazing fell

" Down at the feet of those devoted twain

" The ladder, sole escape from out the abyss.

" With horror-stricken eyes we saw them stand

" To us uplifted, who could help no more;

" Then rush along the broken ground below

" 'Mid fiery flake and smoking ash, for so

" Doubtless they hoped by the other shafts to win

" Some outlet ; but we know that could not be.

" So they were lost.   Your grief excels not ours ;

" For Dennell was esteemed among the first,

" In skill and courage, of our officers."

Then Conway said, " Your answer wounds me sore."

And further question he would fain have put,

But now the other beckoned one hard by ;

" Lingers yet any in the shaft ? " he said.

" None, captain ; none could longer stay and live ;

" Demons of whirlwind, and fierce flame, and death

" Sole revellers make sport in those vast halls—

" Now made a hell—where yesterday we toiled."

To him the captain answered thus in turn :

" Now must we haste to close the shafts ; for so

" The flame shall lack its windy nutriment.

" Hammick, the task is thine ; see thou 'tis done

" With care exact, and let the workers draw

" Long beams across each several mouth, and weave

" The whole with matted twigs together fast,

" And pile a layer of dense earth above ;

" Then drench with water—keep it ever moist.

" And first, the shaft whereby we made ascent ;

" This, that caught last, blazes most fiercely now ;
" With that begin, the rest in order due."
And Hammick answered, " Ay, it shall be done,
" But 'tis the sealing of a sepulchre.
" The mine is lost; none shall descend it more."
But angrily the captain turned on him :
" What ! dost thou argue? 'tis fine time indeed
" For questioning ! and is it thine to say,
" What can, what cannot be ?   Quick, make thou speed !
" Take heed the openings are securely closed."
So Hammick took departure, and again
The captain called, " Gelart !" and one drew near.
" Much store of medicine has been lost, consumed
" In burning of the huts.   Thou therefore haste ;
" See without fail that messengers are sent
" To Villa Rica, and inquire in full
" From the physicians, what appliances,
" What drugs, they deem most needful in the strain
" Of this distress ; and strictly be it said,
" All must be sent before this coming day
" Declines to evening.   Be there no delay."
So from another to another still
The captain called, and Conway well perceived
No further answer could be won from him.
So to his daughter turning, he began :
" Sylvia, we do but hinder here, 'tis plain ;
" 'Twere best to hasten back ; and restful sleep.
" You need, which cannot be in this turmoil.
" Come, then.   Antonio with the mules awaits
" A furlong hence.   Ah me ! I did not think,

"When we set out, not twenty hours ago,
"And through the peaceful forest glades rode down,
"We should adventure on such tragedy."
On then they went; but Sylvia held her peace.
Now came to pass a matter slight but strange.
Along the road, and speeding toward the mine,
A man, tall, strong, and resolute of air,
Went by; to whom a voice, unseen and low,
"Ferrara, 'tis prepared." He stayed his step;
Then plunged amid the darkness, and was lost.
And Conway heard a hum and tramp of men
That way, and wondered if aught sinister
Lay in the thing that he had seen and heard,
And afterward remembered it again.
Now presently they reached the last deep mouth
That yawned in earth toward that dread abyss;
All black it lay. Not yet the workers came
To pile their logs, and close it from the air;
But curling wreaths of smoke uprose to heaven,
High, and yet not so dense as heretofore.
Conway drew near, and downward looked. Just then
A light wind bore the outer smoke aside,
And that within the shaft in filmy shreds
Broke up, and so dispersed; and now a cry
Smote from the depth on Conway's ears. With that
He fixed his gaze intently, but the void,
Blacker than blackest night, revealed not aught;
And yet again the cry was upward borne.
Now beside Conway stood the muleteer,
Who from his wallet drew a lantern forth,

Struck seeds of fire, and lit the torch within ;
Then with the penetrating ray explored
The shaft's down-stretching sides, till fell the light
Upon two forms, one standing and one prone,
Round whom the eddying smoke now surged, and then
Dissolved again, and left them plain to view.
A stony heap upheld them, but below
Sloped into darkness ; and among the stones
Rent beams were mixed, and twisted bars of iron
Fallen from the sides, that from above o'erhung ˙
Hollow and threatening ; so no foot of man,
How skilled soe'er and cunning, could win hold
And climb to th' upper air and solid earth.
Like an inverted funnel fell the gulf
Downward.   But on the verge where Conway stood
Two solid posts upreared were fixed secure ;
Therefore with haste the muleteer unwound
A rope, that in the baggage was upcoiled,
And round one pillar with firm tightened folds
Drew it ten times, and with a twisted knot
Fastened, then let the unrolling length of cord
Fall gently down, until it reached the twain.
He that was standing seized it, and disposed
About his fallen comrade ample length
Beneath the armpits, and made firm the knot ;
So was he first drawn up, and Conway turned
The lantern's light upon him hastily.
Lo ! in that shape, that seemed as motionless
As death, full well Conway and Sylvia knew
Dennell.   A deep-drawn breath, the while they looked,

K

Showed him alive; a scarf his temples bound,
Therefrom the blood had welled; and clotted gore
Clung to his cheek, mingled with dust and sand.
His eyes just opened and then closed again.
Some shattering mass had struck and laid him low;
The bleeding wound his comrade had essayed
To staunch with hasty bandage. But by this
The rope was laden with its second freight;
By dint of sinewy muscle, straining hard,
They bore a heavier burden than the first
Up to the brink, a negro, brawnylimbed;
Scanty his garb—a rough coarse cloth alone
Girded his waist and loins. But Sylvia ran
To where a little runnel gently leapt
Down the slant field, and with the clear cold wave
Filled to the brim a cup, and cleansed the cheek
And brow of Dennell, and withdrew the scarf
With softer kerchiet binding round his head,
And moistened now and yet again his lips,
So parched and dry, with water freshly drawn.
He breathed anon, and stirred; yet heeded not
What passed around, nor heard the voice of friends.
Then Sylvia : " Father, it were much amiss
" To leave him here.   There is no quiet spot,
" Nor any home that can receive him now;
" Confusion all.   The medicine stores are burnt.
" Were it not better he should stay awhile
" On the cool hill-top 'neath the forest boughs,
" Under the roof that we this morning left,
" The kind physician's, who with tender care

" Will bring him to recovery?   See, the night
" Is but an hour beyond the parting line
" Of day and day, and we can win the hill
" Before the sun attains his sweltering power ;
" And all the way, when once the plain is passed,
" Is shadowed by thick trees."   And Conway thus
Answered : " 'Twere best indeed.   Antonio here
" Will help to bear him ; will you not, my friend?
" You shall have treble payment for to-day,
" And more, if well you speed.   And see, there lies
" A hurdle near, and we will weave a couch
" Of rushes ; and his comrade from the pit,
" Saved sound, will aid, who also will return
" To-morrow and bear news that he is safe,
" If safe he is."   Through Conway's mind a thought
Glanced quickly then : " My merchant's craft has long
" Needed a man like Dennell, skilled and brave ;
" If he recover, as I trust full well,
" My service he shall enter, and therein
" Find ampler profit than he e'er can reap
" From these fire-breathing bowels of the earth."
So laid they Dennell gently on soft couch,
And bore him on along the darkling way ;
And Conway plied with questions, as they went,
The swarthier bearer of the wounded man,
How he and Dennell clomb their fearful way
Out of that furnace ; and in broken words,
Now English, now in tongue of Portugal,
And gestures interspersed where language failed,
The other told his tale ; how Dennell led

By cognizance of passage, crack, and turn,
Or ledge that scaled the seeming pathless walls
Up the fourth shaft, that first had caught the fire,
And smouldered now in smoke, which in the gorge,
Where most it narrowed, choked them nigh to death ;
And how their skin was shrivelled with the heat,
Which, were it not that watery floods outpoured
Here only had some quenching coolness brought,
Surely had quite consumed them ; how at last,
Gaining the summit of the stony pile,
They saw through wreaths of dense or lessening smoke
The hollow sides impending frown, that so
No foot could climb ; and waiting here with eyes
Strained to the rift above, a mighty mass
Falling had overwhelmed them, earth and stone ;
And he had 'scaped unhurt, he knew not how,
But rising from the dust and stunning crash
Saw Dennell prone, and stricken nigh to death.
And Conway wondering heard.   But now the stars,
Whose bright eyes glimmered through the leaves o'erhead,
Began to yield, and day o'erspread the woods.
The wounded man, more restless, tossed and moaned ;
So were they glad to reach the friendly house,
Where in clean bed by careful hands disposed
Quiet he lay, save for the throbbing dart
And heat of fever in his veins unquelled.
Three months he lay in sickness, able scarce
To lift his hand, and slowly gathered strength.
And Conway in that kindly home remained
For yet a week with Sylvia.   Then he needs

Must journey home, and Sylvia begged to join
In that return, and said her health was won.
Truly her father marvelled seeing her ;
Calm was her mien, and all unrest dispelled.
He doubted if 'twould last, and so demurred ;
Yet lastly yielded.   Sylvia sought her home.

Now, on the morrow of the day whereon
They carried Dennell through the darkling woods,
Had Conway framed a letter, which should tell
The captain that was chief o'er all the mine
All that had happened—how his comrade lay
Alive, though sorely hurt, within the lodge
Upon the cool and forest-covered hills.
And this the negro taking, pledged his faith
Truly to render to the captain's hand ;
But on the road he met a runaway
Of his own kin, who with persuasion wrought
So much upon him, and with hope held out
Of liberty, that, swerving from the way,
He wandered southward, and forgot his trust,
And nevermore beheld the mine again.
And Dennell was accounted dead, and thus
Report was sent to England.   Her it reached
Who most must grieve.   On Helen's ear and heart
And inmost soul the fatal message fell.

The chord that trembled with Love's music erst
    Is silenced, rent in twain,

As when beneath Atlantic billows first
    The lightning-dowered chain

Bore speech of man from wondering shore to shore,
    But then was stricken dumb,
Marred in mid-ocean ; so to these no more
    The mutual word can come.

Nigh death is he, she deems him dead indeed ;
    O mists of ignorance !
Though fate should spare, yet frailty may mislead,
    Or guile, or aimless chance.

Seek they to taste of that immortal fruit
    Which flattered them erewhile,
Now must they tread the pathless desert mute,
    Uncheered by sign or smile ;

And for refreshment of their thirst must bear
    (Beneath the parching ray)
The springs of faith ; but ah, what faith shall dare
    Foretell the happier day ?

For if the heart once tire, 'tis not as wood
    Or stone or brass or steel,
Wherein the flaw, though long it may have stood,
    A cunning hand may heal ;

But sacred hope once wounded dwindles fast
    Through rivals that assail.
Shall youth's pure passion wear the crown at last,
    Or battling fall and fail?

Now leave we that far region of the West,
Dennell, yet lying on his fevered couch ;
Peranne, in patience sad and resolute ;
Ferrara, and the fierce conspiracy ;
And be it still untold, if from the mine
(Whose flaming ruin he had subtly caused)
He drew a liberated band, to march,
Vanguard of armies, o'er the shaken land,
Subverting rule.   To English shores we turn,
To Helen 'mid the hills of Westmoreland,
And him who called her daughter.

       It was said
What vast design engaged Dundas of old ;
And like that spider famed in history,
Whose web seven times was ruined and renewed,
Or like the king who took example thence,
He from his hour of first calamity
Had laboured on, nor yielded of his hope.
Only his minished wealth no more retained
That sway o'er things material, which could show
The brain's high phantasies in very act
Embodied ; so the common herd, who judge
By what they see, were left undazzled still.
To win the fruit of thought he must become
Suppliant to others ; and with fevered zeal,
By suasion, reasoning, proof, and document,
In many a merchant's chamber he would urge
The glittering prize, whereof the key was held
By him alone ; but sceptic, hard, and dry
The listeners sat.   At last one summer's day

A message came like zephyr in soft spring
Loosening from foggy frost the lifeless ground ;
From France it came, and bore the seal of one
High in the splendour of the imperial court,
And hope was offered that Dundas should bask
Beneath those smiles august and dominant.
Only for gold, for gold ! was still the cry.
Initiation into that fair realm
Was bought with Dennell's gift.   Then charges grew ;
For though at last an empire might sustain
The Atlantean burden, yet Dundas
Must share the load till sure success appeared.
Impetuous now he probed the springs of wealth,
But liked not any.   Casting then his eyes
On those ancestral lands, his pride so long,
But hindrance rather since misfortune came,
Draining his treasure and untrimmed withal,
He thought a sudden thought, and made resolve
Sharply, and spoke to Helen :

　　　　　　　　" Thou hast known,
" Daughter, my toil for many a year, and helped
" My purposes, according to thy strength.
" Now shalt thou be partaker more in full
" Of my intents, and aid the arduous choice
" Which lies before us.

　　　　　　　" Helen, you have seen
" The magnet's force upon the answering steel,
" And how the steel may win that force, and rule
" O'er other fragments not participant
" In that pervasive thrilling influence ;

" And it may be that you have heard, our earth,

" How dull soe'er it shows in clod or stone,

" Doth teem with that same power, and thus responds

" Unto our system's mighty lord, the sun ;

" Which things considering I conceived belief

" That out of every substance can be drawn

" This wondrous potency, and made to serve

" The use of man.   Through what long doubt and hope

" The quest was made, it needs not I should say.

" Suffice it, I have found the secret clue ;

" And I could multiply and concentrate,

" Beyond all thought, this power, with such effect

" In war or peace, that whosoever wields

" The aid I bring, would be of all mankind

" Acknowledged master.

                " But, alas, howe'er

" I hold this knowledge, Helen, scope and means

" Fail me for operation ; and not one

" Of all my countrymen has enterprise

" (So cold their blood) to join with me herein

" And reap the harvest of this toil sublime.

" Shall I give in, and basely rest and rust ?

" That will not I.   One road remains— to seek

" In foreign lands the aid my own denies ;

" In France I hear of those whose mind is tuned

" To high invention.   Thither we will go ;

" And for all needs I have resolved to sell

" My house and land.   Boldly to cast the die

" Is wisdom in due season ; and yourself,

" Helen, will be enlarged in soul and sense

" By sight of ancient cities, famous lands——
" What, do you weep, my child ? "
For Helen's tears

Flowed suddenly. That dear and ancient home,
Before her eyes and deeper in her heart,
To lose it and to see it nevermore,
Where happiness had been so much, so long;
The golden days of childhood ; memories,
Like tender fledglings, now to be disturbed
From their soft nest, adrift in the rude world,
Haply to perish, lacking sustenance
Of present sight.   Then flashed a sudden dread,
Lest merciless blind chance with lightning stroke
Should scathe the clue that linked her to her love
By message rare but sure ; and then she feared
Some nameless ill of wild adventure born
Striking her father.   " Father," she replied,
" Are we not happy here ?   O let us rest !
" It frightens me, as though we set our feet
" Upon the loose edge of a precipice,
" To think of leaving these sweet ways of home
" In search of greatness.   Stay on England's soil.
" I will do all a daughter can for you,
" More zealous will I be than heretofore,
" And aiding you will be my happiness.
" Only forsake not peace for dangerous ways."
But with a touch of irritable scorn,
And yet not roughly, answered her Dundas :
" Helen, you know not that whereof you speak ;
" I might have known you would shrink back.   But I

" Must onward, and I seek no counsellor.
" There is a time for individual choice,
" When threads of action are so finely twined
" That he alone, whose destined deed is ripe,
" Can judge the end.   And that is so with me ;
" Beyond your judgment is my purpose fixed,
" And if you speak of aiding me, then trust
"What I have willed ; 'twere better so by far
" Than idly fret and shed these hindering tears."
And when she knew his will so strongly set,
And knew the day of their departure thence
Was distant yet so far, that written lines
From Dennell's hand would surely meet her eye
(For so she deemed) ere that unwished-for dawn,
Then Helen ceased.   But in her heart no sign,
Nor hint of fear, nor vague imagining,
Rose of another sadder earlier day,
That should make light the pang of severance
From the fair haunts of home, and looks of friends.

For now the direful tidings fell on her
Of Dennell whelmed by flaming death.   Ah, what
Suffers the loving spirit, when the loved
Is into night impenetrable reft,
Divided by a barrier not of steel,
Nor flaming walls, nor spaces of the sea,
But merest silence ! ah, how many weep
Such loss ! how many, having wept, escape
From burning grief to cold oblivion's flood,
And drink life-lessening peace ! but Helen, no.

Sweet breathed the breath of morn, and sweetly she
In household ways that hour was ministering
About her father ; blithe her speech, and blithe
A catch of song she trilled for pure delight,
Like natural fountain flowing merrily ;
When he : "The tidings I have read but now,
" Helen, will grieve you."   And her prescient soul
Forecast the tale that had not reached her ear.
Pale did she stand, and heard the sum of ill.
Dundas, who lacked not love for her, howe'er
In his own quest and anxious thought absorbed,
Strove by diversion of her grief to soothe,
But vainly, as is ever so ; for they
Who thus are grieved cling closer to their grief,
As if therein were very bliss enshrined.
And little did she answer him, or speak,
Nor wept a tear ; but afterward alone,
She wept full many a tear upon her bed,
And in that glen so full of memories ;
And when for weeping she could weep no more,
And eyes and throat were dry, she rose and went
To one that was her foster-mother once
In helpless infancy, who ne'er had ceased
To love the maiden, and rejoice in her
As of all maidens best and loveliest.
There, in the lowly cottage, wreathed in sprays
Of rose and fuchsia, Helen sat and told
(Clasping the listener's hand) from first to last
All that of Henry Dennell she had known ;
Nor wept, nor sobbed, but plaintively spoke on,

As if she loved to speak, and could not bear
To leave the dear-loved theme, but must renew
Each memory till it had the stamp of words
So to be surer held ; and slowly then
Divinely moving waves of comfort crept,
Tokens of living essences, that are
Not of our earthly substance, but inspire
Knowledge—we know not how—and formless life,
And warmth that ne'er had kindling from the sun.
The stricken heart must tell its wound, or die ;
Truly 'twas said ; and Helen spoke, and lived.

And Helen wrote two letters in those days.
The first, to him who ruled the mine of gold ;
Of him she made request, that he should tell
How Henry Dennell died.   And answer came
Duly ; and o'er and o'er she conned each phrase,
And most the words that touched upon the worth
And courage of her lost, her dear betrothed ;
As sacred record did she treasure them.
The second was to Dennell's mother writ,
For consolation and for duty's sake,
And further cause besides ; and thus it ran—
" Mother of him who was your heart's delight,
" Long years ere he became the joy of mine,
" Whom now we weep together, yes, together,
" Though far apart in body, and though ne'er
" Our eyes may meet or voices interchange
" Our deep sad thoughts by utterance ; this, at least,
" I needs must send ; oh, would it worthier were

" To carry comfort, as indeed it bears
" Reverence ; and that was due before, and paid
" By tribute of my heart, and now at last
" My pen may write it ; grief unseals the truth.
" O that my grief could lighten yours ! but now
" 'Tis I to you must be a suppliant ;
" For it may be that you can tell me things
" About my Harry, that I have not known,
" And most in this last year ; for 'tis a year
" Since last, according to our mutual pledge,
" Preserving reverence for my father's will,
" He sent me words, the dearest gift of time,
" From that far land.   But tell me now, I pray,
" What more 'tis right and good that I should learn."
And Dennell's mother sent reply ; and thus
Did Helen learn how Dennell found the vein
Of hidden gold, and afterward the gift
He made her father.   Ah, what feelings stole
Upon her ! wonder first, and awe's sad thrill,
At strength by fortune crowned, by death undone ;
And all the air, the room wherein she sat,
Seemed full of him ; then echoes of his voice
Flitted and shook the chord of grief within,
With blank desire, fond memory, vanished hope ;
The goal by him so near attained, yet lost ;
Life's fruitless quenching ; so the circuit ran.
But this was ere she saw her father's name ;
Now did she read and understand the words
That told of Dennell's gift ; a sudden shock
Ran through her pulses ; anger filled her blood.

All day in troubled thought she moved ; at eve,
More calm, she spoke.   " My father, answer me.
" Is it not true, that Henry Dennell paid
" A portion of the debt his father owed ? "
" Whence knew you that?"   he cried, and something
    sharp
Rang in his tone ; but she was stirred thereby
To sudden scorn and wrathful irony ;
" Whence knew I that ? a generous question.   True,
" With Harry Dennell I had no concern ;
" 'Twas you had dealings with him, and you reached
" A rare degree of amity therein ;
" So when he offered from his poor estate
" This recompense of ills he had not done,
" 'Twas yours to take it ; friend may take from friend ;
" It was not mine to know what he had done.
" Nay, now, when he is dead and in his grave,
" His far unhonoured grave, forlorn and drear,
" That never may be watered by the drops
" From those sad eyes that ever weep and love,
" Nor strewn with flowers by hands that met his clasp
" So joyously of old ; when nought is left,
" Save to recall, repeating o'er and o'er,
" How brave, how gentle ;—this you suffer not ;
" Your ears are sealed, I cannot speak to you ;
" And having such a matter in your thoughts
" As should have stirred your tenderness for him
" Who dealt so nobly by you, this you keep
" Secret and silent ; oh, ungenerous ! "
Now was Dundas at these accusing words

Somewhat ashamed and in his conscience pricked,
But not for long ; he rallied strength and spoke :
" You misconceive me, Helen, utterly.
" Since you possess this knowledge (and it seems
" I may not question whence you gathered it),
" I am not greatly sorry ; yet, indeed,
" I thought and think it somewhat dangerous ;
" For 'tis not possible, you must allow,
" That you should look with such impartial eyes
" On Henry Dennell as another might ;
" Though you are good, my Helen ; but in truth
" I deemed it better that you should not know.
" And till this last sad news (that moved your grief
" So deeply and so justly) 'tis most sure
" And certain, had I told you of this thing,
" You would have claimed with absolute demand
" The restoration of the link that once
" Had been approved, in times far different ;
" Which now I could not sanction.   But perchance
" I may have erred since then, and since his death
" It had been better to have told you all.
" Be it an error, if you will ; and yet
" To blame too harshly must appear in you
" Strange self-regard and strange severity."
Then Helen was thrown back, and half accused
Herself in turn.   With quiet voice at last
She spoke : " Our difference is of old herein.
" 'Tis sharp as black from white, as night from noon.
" As though a gulf divided us, and we
" Scarce heard each other's voices borne across,

"So was it and so is it.   But with time
" Right judgment comes.   I would not now complain ;
" I am too much your debtor in all else ;
" As daughter, and for that unfailing care
" You showed my childhood.   But I may not now
" Flatter ; this only I would ask beyond—
" Say this at least, that he of whom we speak
" Had, more than most, an honest, generous soul ;
" And that you have in nought been harmed by him,
" Neither by me through him."   He answered then,
" That he was honest, Helen, I allow ;
" And few are honest.   For your further claim,
" I needs must urge, he was made generous
" By hope of recompense.   He harmed me not ;
" I never charged him with my injuries."
But Helen feared, lest aimless strife should grow.
" Enough," she said ; " your bidding and request
" Alone shall make me speak of him henceforth."
And rising, she departed.   All that night
A wakeful anger surged, and tossed her heart,
Like some poor ship o'er which the wild waves yawn ;
And e'en the thought came over her to leave
The father so unjust, so harsh, and choose
Some purpose, which the wondering world might deem
Love's kindly fruit ; but tender old constraint
Returning won her back, and that resolve
Of patience ; and no seeming way of good
Equalled the task she held to aid her sire ;
That way her duty still unbroken lay.
So with the morn she drew the breath of peace.

And now Dundas his patrimony sold ;
The house, the garden, and the hillside wood,
Where gushed the brooklet cool o'er mossy stones ;
The field, that upward sloped unevenly,
Besprent with mounds, peaceful with browsing kine ;
Yea, and each little thing that use made dear
To Helen's heart—the sun-dial on the lawn,
The clock upon the stairs, the sofa, wrought
In antique style, with subtle carving quaint,
And many an old familiar ornament.
Day flowed on day, the latest morning shone,
Increased to noon, and then the parting came ;
They left the roof that ne'er should know them more.

O wherefore on the hills
Linger my feet beneath the summer skies,
   When he, whose image fills
My lonely heart, is lost to these sad eyes ?

   Dear hills, I must depart
From you for aye ; and that I must, is well ;
   More sacred in my heart,
Entwined with him, so shall you ever dwell ;

   With him, who in this glade
Pledged me sweet faith in the hour of love's bright morn ;
   With him, who now is laid
In sad strange tomb, in caves of night forlorn.

O stream ! if ever he,
In that immortal vesture clad, should seek
 Thy banks for love of me,
And thou to his fine sense attuned canst speak,

 Tell him of these hot tears
Wept in thy wave, the sighs I sigh to-day ;
 Tell him, through lifelong years
I seek him ; tell him, I am his alway.

 Seaward my tears descend,
Where lies their kindred flood ; but heavenly fire
 Is of my course the end ;
There shall I mingle with my heart's desire.

 Dear ancient friends, I go ;
Ye smile on me, soothing my lonely pain.
 O my lost love !   I know,
Thee yet once more with these I shall regain.

In London first, not many days, Dundas
Sojourned with Helen.   Paris afterward
Received their homeless feet ; and their abode
In that bright city month on month was set,
From dusk November till the burning eve
Of August.   'Twas the last and lurid hour,
When seeds of ruin gathered in the air
To burst in tempest on that dynasty

Born of a nation's fear and pride, and slain
By their contempt; but now the bolt of death
Slumbered, and those doomed palaces upreared
To smiling heavens their scatheless splendour still.
But he that wore the imperial crown, impelled
By deep dark bodings, cast about his hands
(Like swimmer seaward borne on ebbing tides,
Fainting, and past his strength, with terror's clutch
Seizing each casual thing) to find some prop
That should support him till the perilous hour
Was overpast; full many a lure was thrown,
And scheme was schemed, and dazzling show devised,
And weapon forged for secret swift assault;
So it befell, Dundas in favour grew
With favourites of that tottering throne, as one
Whose keen invention might be turned to help;
Glorious with hope and pride he budded out,
And clean forgot a sin that vexed his soul
When first he sinned it.
                  For upon the morn
Whereon they left the vales of Westmoreland,
A letter, superscribed with Helen's name,
Was brought; she was not near; her father marked
That from Brazil it came, and wondered more,
Knowing the hand that wrote.   In strange unrest
He murmured then, " From Dennell this, to-day !
" How has it come? mislaid, perhaps, of old ;
" A friend has sent it, since himself is dead.
" Or lives he still? I needs must know ; but she—
" Is it so well that it should meet her eye ?

" Another life henceforth begins for us."
He broke the seal, and read the words that ran
Trembling, awry, and signed with letters twain.
" Sweet love, I have been hurt ; 'tis over now,
" And I am better ; write to me ; farewell."
Dundas, though all absorbed in vast designs,
So that he grudged the hours of rest and food,
Was roused to other thoughts, and mused in pain.
Not gladly would he have deceived his child,
But was it then deceit ? and Dennell's gift
Had softened, but not quelled, the ancient grudge ;
At length he folded up and hid the lines
'Neath lock and key, and whispered inwardly ;
" If at this hour I should reveal this thing
" To Helen, in the sudden stress of joy
" She will o'erpower me with her prayers and tears ;
" And then ? it well may happen, I shall yield ;
" My daughter will be reft away from me,
" And I all lonely left ; or else, at best,
" A matter half forgotten will revive,
" Drag on beyond all reckoning.   Better far
" Is silence in such case ; and Helen's bloom
" Will redden with the blush of joy again .
" In other scenes, by new enchantments lured ;
" So, if the youth persist not, all is well ;
" If he persist, the question can be solved
" Some other day.   'Tis certain that no tongue
" Can give a hint of this to Helen's ear."
He ended so.   A brother came that morn,
Who should have charge of matters whatsoe'er

Concerned Dundas in England afterward;
With him were many things in private conned,
Perused, explained; and then Dundas began
In subtle phrase.

     " Brother, there is a thing
" On which I would entreat your special care.
" You may remember—for your memory keeps
" Its freshness still; my own begins to dull—
" My daughter had a child's engagement once
" Half countenanced by me; in every truth
" 'Twas for brief time allowed.   The youth was son
" Of him whose ruinous collapse you know,
" Dennell; it needs not I should say how much
" Myself was hurt in that calamity.
" After the father's fall, it was not meet
" The son should wed my daughter; in plain terms
" I told him this; with violence he stormed,
" But presently confessed he had no claim
" In his own right.   Yet once or twice since then
" He wrote to Helen, and she answered him;
" I deemed it well to let the matter glide,
" Lest too grave meaning should be set thereon.
" But now this comes to pass.   His work has lain
" (Honest it is, but quite unmarked and poor)
" In a Brazilian mine; but this by fire
" Is ruined, and 'twas said he perished there;
" Now I am glad to find that is not true.
" But since he is so passionate and rash
" (Although, I frankly grant, not void of worth),
" I fear (and more from something lately heard)

" Lest in his straits he wildly sue again
" For Helen's hand.   A grievous harm were here ;
" Helen is happy, save for leaving home ;
" She leads with me a busy useful life,
" And pays me every dutiful regard,
" And is a pearl of daughters, I may say ;
" It were a pity if her tranquil mind
" Were to be shaken, and ta'en back to thoughts
" Which cannot lead to any useful end.
" Have then a care, if he should ask of you,
" How you acquaint him with my dwelling-place.
" Yet, brother, misconceive me not herein.
" I would have knowledge, should he chance to come
" Beneath your keen eyes' notice, face to face,
" Of all concerning him—his aspect, mien,
" Fortune, and present tasks.   I say not this
" As minded to allow his suit to Helen,
" But I should wish to keep him in my view.
" And if he seek to write, restrain him not ;
" Send me his letter.   Use all care, I pray ;
" If Helen met with him, grave harm might come."
And John Dundas had promised to take heed
And use all caution in the thing required.
But yet for many a day Dundas was loth,
After that hour, to look on Helen's eye ;
And feared, his blameless child might see in him
A hidden guile ; and walked with guarded mien.

But now in Paris fortune shone, and drove
Old thoughts away, like clouds when rain is o'er ;

Then jauntily he stepped and freely spoke,
And men began to look on him as one
Noted for strong intelligence, and framed
For princes' favour ; and the rumours grew
Of some new art his zeal and skill had found.
But Helen clad herself in sad attire,
And served her father with grave quietness ;
And wondered often what should be the end,
And if herself should e'er again be glad ;
For old familiar talk was lessened now,
And silence burdened.   Once she named the name
Of him, the lost ; for trial's sake perchance ;
But something froze her in her father's look,
She knew not why.   Meantime her 'customed task
Lay in his service, as in olden time.
But such unwonted life, and the hot glare
Of streets, the crowded city's throng and noise,
Besides her inward grief and solitude,
Made thin and pale her cheek, and dimmed her eye ;
And flights of stairs outwearied those firm limbs
To crags and hills inured ; and dazzling nights
In palaces made no amends ; and oft
She wondered at her weakness, and would think,
" What is it that has come to me of late ? "
And then the murmur of her own dear streams
Would ripple through her ears, and mountain winds
Would seem to rustle round her, and the scent
Of pines on fancy's breath be borne, and light
Of purple evening play on moor and crag ;
Yet scarce she knew if she desired return

To those loved scenes, unless a voice could sound
Which now she deemed for ever stilled in death ;
So all her nutriment of heart was set
In barren parching soil ; and gathering ills
Foreboded worse.   Yet outward change was nigh ;
A change to many, past all fancy's range.

For war's fierce lightning flashed, and murky gloom
Rushed down and wrapped the towers and homes of
     France.
O thrust of fire !   O mighty overthrow !
High vaunt, swift ruin ! age-long glories quelled !
But long ere serried foes were seen, or walls
Engirt with flame, or din of bursting bomb,
Dundas foreknew the touch of doom, and took
His way, with Helen, to a southern shore.

She moves as in a dream along
    The glittering halls of pride,
Of wit and mirth and dance and song ;
    But muses sober-eyed.

Lo ! nations into battle start ;
    The cannon thunders swell ;
With awe she hears ; but in her heart
    Two visions only dwell,

The sunlight on the lands behind,
    The gathering gloom of sorrow ;

O shall she through the darkness find
A dawn of joy to-morrow?

———————

Ah, was it so, that never sign or word
Came unto Helen, bearing truth at last?
Came Dennell's message never from afar,
Like arrow to the gold, crying, " I live ;
" I yet am thine ! " or did indeed the stroke
Of fever, rising victor once again,
Tear him from hopes reborn and quickened life?
Not so.   Awakened from the cloudy trance,
Out of whose womb the thronging phantoms swarmed,
Mid fiery pain or dull oppression dim,
Of substance void, by memory unretained,
A rout ungoverned, fleeting, shadowlike ;
Weak as an infant on his bed he lay,
Pleased with the cooling air that kissed his brow,
And sunbeams dancing on the coloured walls ;
Knowing nor caring wherefore he was there ;
Till the physician came.   And Dennell sought
To rise, but strength availed not in his limbs.
Then cried he, " What is this? how came I here?
" I am bewildered."   Manuel (so was named
The kindly healer) answered, " You were hurt,
" But now 'tis well ; your strength returns again."
So hour by hour the quiet day passed by,
And yet another ; but the second night
Bore on her wings a thrilling dream.   It seemed
He stood upon the threshold of his house

Hard by the mine ; the blazing sun was high ;
Then Helen came and spoke the word.   " O love,
" At last our happiness is fixed and sure ;
" Come, let us talk as in the olden days ;
" For all our trouble now is chased away ;
" The ship is in the harbour, and awaits
" Our lagging steps ; delay no more, but seek
" With me the land we love."   And he replied,
" My bride, I come ; I knew not thou wert here."
By this his breast was filled so full of joy,
That e'en awakened he was cheered thereby,
Though spun of fancy's tissue.   Now he heard
And, looking through the open casement, saw
Rain as one mighty torrent-flood descend.
" Is this the stormy quarter of the year,"
He thought, " that verges toward the latter end ?
" What month of all the twelve is o'er me now ?
" Methought the central day was scarcely won ;
" I cannot call to mind that I have writ
" The letter that I purposed ; Helen sure
" Will think I have delayed from idleness ;
" It vexes me ; but I must ask with speed."
Therefore he counted moments, minutes, hours,
Till the physician came ; " Kind sir," he said,
" What month is this ? "   " September," answered he,
" Is at the ending ; 'tis the thirtieth day.
" Three months are gone, and more, since you were
        brought ;
" Conway the merchant hither came with you
" Two days before Saint John's high festival—

" Three hours ere noon ; for I recall it well."
Then Dennell mused.   " I do remember now
" That Conway and his daughter Sylvia came
" Unto my dwelling ; was I hurt that day ? "
" Ay, it was so, indeed."   And Dennell knew
Surely no letter had by him been sent
That year to Helen ; and with trembling hand
He wrote the lines that heretofore were told
(For vainly Manuel's prudent zeal forbade) :
" Sweet love, I have been hurt ; 'tis over now,
" And I am better ; write to me ; farewell."

Manuel to Conway presently sent word,
" The youth wins back his strength ; " and Conway wrote,
How, ere seven days had passed, himself would come
For gratulation's sake, and with intent
To speak of matters touching Dennell's weal.
Dennell by this was moved to ponder much,
And asked and learnt what way his hurt had come ;
Amazed was he, and sorely grieved, to hear
So great disaster ; also now he feared
His office should be lost.   But Manuel spoke :
" Sir, be not over-careful in respect
" Of that your office.   Conway bids me say,
" To stay your cares if you should question thus
" (What he himself will shortly tell you here),
" Seeing the mine is brought so low, he deems
" You may accept an honourable post
" That he can offer ; be at rest thereon."
So Dennell slept that hour in quietness.

And Conway came, and Sylvia too, ere long ;
And converse passed ; and he, the wounded man,
First on that day descending from sick bed
To taste heaven's freshness, thanked with grateful word
His kindly helper, and in twice ten days
Promised a sure reply concerning that
Which Conway offered, saying he must needs
Visit the mine once more.   And then he asked
Of all that had been wiped away and lost
From memory's record ; and he marvelled much,
Hearing as new what things himself had done.
But now his thought to other channel turned.
" Whence grew this thing ? knows any man the cause ?
" Came such calamity by chance alone ? "
And Conway answered, " 'Twas a deed of guilt.
" Fanatic passion swells, like seething yeast,
" In this our day ; and there are those who strive
" To free the slave, and build the edifice
" Of equal right, on ruins of the state.
" Such men have plotted in one night to raise
" An army of the Afric blood, conjoined
" With neediest men of Europe's progeny.
" In divers parts the keen assault was planned ;
" In chief, against your mine."
                              But Dennell cried :
" Great Heavens ! and what the end ? "   " The tale is
        short,"
Conway made answer.   " They that planned revolt
" Erred by an over-reckoning of their friends
" Among the Afric race, and 'tis believed

" They better knew the Amazonian shore,
" Where fiercer and more linked by kindred blood
" The slaves are found ; but here in character,
" In tongue, in habit, they among themselves
" Differ ; so union failed.   This much I know ;
" But what befel the night we left the mine,
" Until this hour I have not learnt in full ;
" Though something sinister I did myself
" Behold as we departed."   Dennell then :
" Was any known of those that thus conspired ? "
And Conway : " One alone was named to me,
" Ferrara ; known, 'tis said, in Rio well ;
" A man of ardent brave fanaticism,
" More open than the rest.   He now has fled.
" But one of darker mould and fiercer will
" Behind him stood, who, rumour held of late,
" Was on a sudden slain by private foe
" In casual strife, 'mong those who followed him.
" And most, by caution veiled, and scattered far,
" Pass from remembrance, while the public weal
" Hangs upon nearer matters."   " Strange it is,"
Dennell replied ; " last year, in middle June,
" Being in Rio, on some duty bound,
" At eventide I sat within a house
" Of entertainment ; sitting there I heard
" The casual talk of two who marked me not
" Concerning one whose name until this hour
" I had forgotten ; you have called it back—
" Ferrara.   And they say he plotted much
" For freedom of the slaves."   Then Sylvia spoke :

" Think you such purpose was not honourable ? "
She trembled, for she thought upon Pcranne ;
She guessed, howe'er she spurned the fouler charge
Cast on his name, the temper of his soul
Might from Ferrara not be quite estranged.
" Tut, girl ! " her father answered hastily ;
" False honour dyes full many a villain's cloak."
" And you, what say you ? "   Sylvia turning spoke
To Dennell.   He with slow response at last :
" Some men there are, whom justice dooms to die,
" And yet they must be deemed not wholly base ;
" Their deed is deadly, but their thought is life ;
" And this Ferrara may be one of these."
And Sylvia seemed content ; but Conway cried,
" Nay, lawful ways alone bear honest fruit.
" Men say, the assembly shortly will decree
" That freedom shall be natural heritage
" Of each man born thenceforward in the land.
" Such purpose may you honour ; not the mind
" Of reinless zealots."   Soon the theme was changed.
Conway and Sylvia from the hills next day
Descended to the city by the sea.

———

Whate'er thou deem'st on earth
     Most evil, scan it well,
A buried seed of worth
     Doth surely in it dwell ;

Though every voice combined
In honour of thy ways,
A something wilt thou find
To mend in after days.

———

Dennell with secret pleasure in his heart
Thought upon Conway's offer; who had said
He needed one of judgment and resolve
More than exact preciseness in the lore
Of merchant's craft; and one that could control
Large matters, stretching over land and sea.
So gracious phrase with timely help was joined;
Nor failed, like fostering rain on soil long dry,
The cheering sense, that now his enterprise
Would reach to England, now Dundas would know,
And melodies of ancient hope would fall
On Helen's ear.   Yet ere th' intent could grow,
He needs must journey to the mine once more.
Down through the woodland glades at dawn he rode;
And where the woodland ended, found as erst
The little inn (howbeit the folk were new),
And stabled there his steed; then pacing o'er
The arid plain familiar to his eyes
(Pale, scarred, and all unlike himself of old),
Ere he could wonder and lament the brand
By fiery whirlwind ruinously stamped
On shaft, machine, and trim white edifice,
Behold ! a negro, by the roadside fixed

Staring, with mouth agape and trembling lips,
Turned suddenly to flight, as seized with fear
Passing endurance ; and a little group,
Remoter, thrilled with some strange sense, drew back ;
Next, Dennell knew the English face of him
That came along ; but Gelart stayed his step,
And pale with low voice spoke : " What name is thine ? "
" You know me ; Dennell." " Dennell ! and alive ! "
" Ay, and alive." " And how ? " But Dennell stood
Himself in wonder steeped past words, past thought.
" How ? knew you not ? deemed you I should refrain
" Returning hither, soon as strength sufficed ?
" Or was it told, my sickness led to death ? "
" Nay, how escaped you from the burning gulf ? "
" Rescued I was, and breathe the breath of life ;
" And was assured, you had been told thereof;
" But for the scene and manner, all is lost
" From my remembrance ; only this was said,
" Out of the fallen ruins I was drawn
" By ropes to th' upper air, and afterward
" By careful tendance on the forest hills
" Safe from the fever of my wounds was brought
" To strength again, as here you see to-day."
" Great Heavens ! this passes wonder," Gelart cried.
" We heard not aught of this ; we saw you pent
" In fiery closure, lost beyond all hope,
" Or so we deemed ; nor any voice, nor breath,
" Nor sign, nor hint, has whispered, Dennell lives :
" What hand, then, saved you ? who could reach you there,
" Sundered by fiery shears from heaven's fair light ? "

Then Dennell answered : " How I clomb the height
" Passes my knowledge ; of myself I clomb,
" Yet by myself I had not saved myself.
" Deliverance came by friendly hands at last ;
" Conway the merchant drew me from the depth.
" But now I fain would know, how fares the mine ?
" What issue from such dire calamity
" For   better   can   be   hoped ? "   " The   loss   strikes
      deep,"
Replied the other, " yet we toil and hope."
Then Dennell : " Seeing you have deemed me dead,
" Another surely fills the place I held ? "
" Myself," said Gelart, " have been so advanced."
Then answered Dennell : " So remain it still.
" Another lot awaits me from this hour ;
" For Conway's service shall I enter now
" And breast the blasts of fate afar from here.
" Though loth am I to leave you in this strained
" And arduous fortune, yet my spirit moves
" To other regions, and the call is given ;
" My labour here is ended.   But I haste
" To see our chief ; for mine I call him yet
" Companion me, if leisure serves, I pray ;
" So these poor folk from sight of you will take
" Courage, who shuddering fly before me now,
" As one escaped, a ghostly shade, from hell."
So Gelart turned with Dennell, and they sought
The chief, who stood with wonder all transfixed,
Nor less, the tale being told.   But Dennell asked,
" Went, then, report to England, I was dead ? "

" Report was sent, as surely we believed.

" And now I call to mind that letters came

" From those in England who esteemed you dear,

" Bedewed with tears, and full of questionings,

" Whereto I answered as I held the truth : "

And then the captain, rising from his seat,

Took from a shelf a volume clasped with brass,

Which duly opened he to Dennell gave ;

" Letters and answer you may here behold."

And Dennell read his father's words, and next

Helen's ; and joy and fear confused his breast ;

Joy at the tenor of her love, but fear

Lest in the fatal cloud of night her faith

Through ignorance should swerve.   So ran his thought,

While slowly through the eyesight to the brain

The answers of his chief made way, and raised

Almost a blush upon his cheek, to read

The praise so given by him who now stood nigh,

To whom he turned and spoke : " I pray you, sir,

" While from my heart I thank you for the words

" That you have shown me, add one kindness more ;

" This—that you send to her, the name you see,

" Helen Dundas, a brief reply again,

" And say that I am living and am well.

" Myself I so have written, but I fear

" Lest accident imperil what I sent ;

" Were I to write again, 'twould trouble her,

" And yet 'tis needful she should know the truth."

Then did the captain smile.   " Ay, ay," he said,

" It shall be done ; and for a recompense,

" Make me a guest upon your wedding day."
And Dennell smiled.   " If e'er that day should come,
" I write you in the tablets of my mind,
" Which shall not be mislaid."   (And be it said,
The captain sent the message ; but Dundas
Dealt with the letter as with Dennell's erst.)
Then Dennell asked, how went that fiery night
Up to the close ; how those had been repelled
Who through such ruin sought to win success
In armed revolt.   Thereto the chief replied .
" Thus runs the tale.   An hour or more had passed
" Since we had mounted to the upper air,
" Leaving our ruined halls the prey of fire,
" When Gelart, who had gone a space of road
" With messengers to Villa Rica sent,
" Saw in returning one with stealthy step
" Creep, bending low, and like a runaway.
" He ran to seize him, but the other fled.
" Gelart, pursuing o'er a brow of hill,
" Found suddenly a throng before his eyes. —
" How many said you ? "   Gelart took the word :
" A hundred I would say, but doubtless more
" Were in the darkness and th' uneven ground
" Hidden.   I knew some swarthy faces there ;
" Others were passing, giving arms to each ;
" And some discerned me, and one called my name,
" And bade me fly.   I fled, and told the tale
" Here to our chief, who best can tell the whole."

" Immediate on the tidings "—thus the chief—

" We sent our men of Afric blood to bide

" Within the huts, save ten or twelve, of brain

" Keener than most, and tried fidelity ;

" These did we send as spies, or counsellors

" Of better course to those that were misled,

" And much good service did we reap thereby.

" But we of European blood kept watch

" All through the night, and waited for the dawn.

" And much persuasion, afterwards we heard,

" Was used by those who had beguiled away

" Our erring men, that they should make assault

" Upon their ancient masters, and break through

" Unto the thousand souls behind our guard

" For perfect liberation of the whole.

" And truly in much danger were we set ;

" But fear, and something of the old esteem,

" Worked in the runaways.　They took their flight ;

" Harried the country for a week with vague

" Uncertain plunder ; then, by chance or plan,

" Meeting some larger bodies like themselves,

" They made a rabble of two thousand men

" Belike or more, which one imperial troop

" With little bloodshed captured or dispersed.

" This was their end ; for us, not any tongue

" Has named despair.　We delve the shaft anew.

" Return you, then, to share our tasks again ? "

But Dennell : " Nay, 'tis settled otherwise.

" Conway the merchant asks that I should take

" Control, in part, of his so wide affairs ;

" Thereto I shall accede.   I leave you now ;
" Yet in remembrance shall I hold the life
" Where first I knew and tried my own hands' strength,
" And with all friendly fancies follow still
" The labour of your hands, till fortune's crown
" Is set upon your purpose."   So with words
Of kindly parting and with wishes given
For mutual weal, and greetings sent to those
Whom Dennell knew but had not seen to-day,
He took departure.   Then beside the wood
Mounting his horse he rode through forest glades
And counted up the time ; " By New Year's dawn
" My Helen's letter will be brought to me."
And as he pondered, Time's far vistas shone
With gathering glories to his inward eye.

But those immortal powers, who gently lead
The human spirit on from the low ground
To swelling hill and sky-wreathed pinnacle,
Are subtler than we deem ; and in their store
Is treasured many a wondrous telescope,
Compact of heavenly crystal, which can show
Some land of light, remote, ethereal, far,
And dim and doubtful to th' unholpen eye,
As though the hand could grasp it where it lies ;
And Dennell found it so.   The winged moons,
Filling the measure of the dying year,
Flew by ; and January passed, devoid
Of hoped for joy ; ay, and with added grief ;
For Dennell's mother had put off the veil

Of earthly being, dying on the day
Whereon she knew her son from death restored.
And strangely mingled were the tones that rang
From that far English home to Dennell's ear,
Of grief and comfort.   But for Dennell grief
Must reign, and for awhile his anxious thought,
Why Helen answered not, was lulled ; his care
Seemed selfishness, but still it grew.   At last
(The year advanced to February now)
He sat one day unhinged in mind, and mused
Whether to speak to any of his load.
" Conway has been the kindest of all friends,"
He thought ; " but inward sorrow suits not well
" With talk of bales and merchants' revenues ; "
So he delayed.   But Conway had perceived
How changed he was and sad, and spoke the first :
" Have you a trouble, Dennell, on your mind ? "
And Dennell knew by speech relief would come ;
And thus began : " Two troubles have been mine.
" The one is sure, the other hangs in doubt ;
" The doubt is sorer far.   My mother died
" Ere last year closed ; the tidings lately came :
" There is no need of many words to tell
" Such grief.   The other calls on me to act ;
" Yet how, I know not.   Ere I left my home,
" A maiden gave her hand and troth to me.
" And for a time her father favoured us ;
" But afterwards my father angered him,
" And so he turned against us, and would fain
" Annul the maiden's troth ; she would not so.

" Once and again she sent me words of love

" Across the ocean ; then she deemed me slain

" In that dread ruin of the blazing mine,

" And wrote, with ne'er-forgetting tender heart,

" Unto my captain of old time, and asked

" Of me, my life and death.   He answered her,

" As he believed.   But now she should have known,

" Ay, long ago, that I am still alive ;

" The fifth month passes since I wrote to her ;

" I looked to have reply by New Year's dawn.

" Also the captain wrote a second time,

" Giving reversal of his former tale.

" Why is she silent ?   I conjecture much :

" She travels, or expects some special thing

" Of weighty import ; if my letter erred,

" E'en though the captain's hit the mark aright,

" 'Twould cause some tarrying.   All may yet be well ;

" But yet the trouble is a trouble still."

Now Conway answered not at once, but stood

In thought ; then questioned more.   At last he spoke :

" Dennell, I have in mind to trust you more

" Than caution in th' extreme would ratify ;

" But since you have been faithful in all else,

" I will not stint you of my confidence.

" Listen.   An aged man, of kin to me,

" Has died in England ; and his will assigns

" To me his whole estate, not over large,

" And yet too large for one to hold it light.

" But now I learn, his tenure of the whole

" Stays not unchallenged ; and by his defect,

" If so 'twere judged, the whole would pass from me,
" Lacking all right unless through him alone.
" Therefore my purpose was, myself to sail
" For England, and to guard the right I have ;
" And yet for many causes I was loth
" To leave this land.   Now, holding all in view,
" I would commission you with this employ,
" To stand in place of me, and keep my weal
" Secure from wrongful force or treacherous fraud.
" Being in England, you might satisfy
" Your private need.   Be this alone made clear,
" That my affair is chief ; nor must you lack,
" From favour to yourself, a point of zeal,
" Whereby my interest may stand secured.
" My kinsman's lawyer will advise aright
" Your general course, and wheresoe'er he guides,
" To him your ear must hearken, and your hand
" Be prompt to act ; but yet some weighty things
" For your determination will abide.
" Take thought, and say if you accept the charge."

Dennell for joy could scarce reply ; but soon
Sought further knowledge ; lastly gave assent.
And Conway deemed, he should within a month
Take ship for England.   But in truth the time
Was longer drawn, and April in mid course
Saw his departure from the western world.

CANTO IV

THE SEARCH FOR HELEN.

O NOW is the conflict approaching, and brief are the
    hours ;
O fill me, enkindle with courage, ye heavenly powers !

Though boom of the cannon resound not, or lance
    glitter bright,
Yet spirit with spirit shall wrestle with straining of might ;

And victory's prize is before me, the splendour above
All splendours in earth or in heaven, the secret of love.

O bride of my heart, shall I find thee my own as of old,
And feel thy warm tender embraces my bosom enfold ?

With me wilt thou stem the wild surges that thunder and
    roar
Against the frail bark of our fortune, far, far, from the
    shore ?

For then were I crowned ; but ah, have I too fondly
    believed ?
And thou hast been silent ; and shall I awake un-
    deceived ?

O ne'er can it be ; for remembrance with trial and quest
Can find in thee nought unbeseeming the purest and
   best ;

The pulses that tremble within me, the thrilling of fear,
Are but as the whisper that tells me why thou art so dear ;

And soon shall these eyes look upon thee in lustre of
   light,
As star in new glory emerging from clouds of the night.

Fly, then, ye swift moments, and bear me o'er ocean's
   great tide
To where my dear fatherland raises his billow-worn side ;

Whose mountains engird the sweet valley of woodland
   so green,
Where wanders in beauty the maiden, of maidens the
   queen.

The ship that carried Dennell o'er the main
Met stormy winds and was delayed thereby ;
So when he landed, middle June was past,
And London squares were green with fullest leaf
Of towering planes.   And first he sought his home,
Hard by the mighty city ; there he saw
One sad sweet day arise and fade to eve,
While of his mother's death he heard ; and long
And dear the converse ; they that yet remained,

Father and sister, told the sudden stroke
That snatched her life ; and childhood's years were
   scanned
In wistful memory ; how she moved, and spoke ;
And it was said, her son was in her thoughts
Ever ; and Dennell wept to hear of it,
And they with him.   But with the second morn
Dennell must needs embark with instant care
On Conway's weighty matter ; day by day
Saw him unresting, for the time was scant ;
Precious the weeks that had been lost at sea.
The days of June wore on ; like bow on strain,
He held in pause the arrow of his will,
Though fretting sore ; then with an arrow's speed
Released he sought the vales of Westmoreland.
The village lay before him in the sun ;
The house beyond, stately, and standing clear,
With lawns in front that merged on forest land ;
And up the hills the forest clomb ; behind
Was one loved glen.   How fresh, how changeless shone
Nature's sweet face ! and all unchanged the heart
In Dennell beat ; and surely now, he deemed,
Should Helen's eyes look on him soon, and he
Gaze upon hers ; and if that ancient grudge,
Nursed by her father, were not laid to rest,
Still might it softer move.   He passed the gate,
And paced the walk, and stood before the door,
The which was half of glass ; the hall was seen ;
But that was changed ; it was not as of old.
And Dennell marked, and felt a sudden pang ;

Chill doubt, too soon confirmed ! He turned away.
Now did he know that Helen and her sire,
Taking departure ere the year was born,
Had left their land for ever ; one alone
Could tell what soil might be their resting-place,
The brother, John Dundas, whose home was set
In Kendal's vale, at outlet of the hills.
Thither unresting Dennell sped, but found
A week must pass ere John Dundas returned.
The week went by, and Dennell came anew,
But weary with his toil, in London smoke
Endured continuous. Now these two of old
Had met but distantly ; and John Dundas
Had that high mien which breeds not ready talk ;
Askance he looked upon the youth, and bowed
With frigid air, in which 'twere difficult
To say if recognition lay or no
(Yet well he recognized, for keen the glance
That shot beneath the calm and ample brow) ;
And Dennell, undelaying, asked the home
Where now Dundas was living. John Dundas
Answered : " My brother longs for privacy.
" I grieve I cannot satisfy your need.
" Entrust a letter to my hand, and this
" Shall duly reach, and duly win reply."
Dennell replied : " A letter will not serve.
" 'Tis no longer trouble I shall ask of him ;
" Nay, of himself I would not ask an hour—— "
He paused ; he feared to utter Helen's name.
But John Dundas supplied the lack with speed :

" In short, it is his daughter you would see.

" That is the very thing he deprecates.

" You make disturbance in her mind, that else

" Would turn to juster aims ; your lot is cast

" In distant perilous lands, for her unmeet ;

" Your wealth, your station, cannot match with hers."

So did he seek to quell the youth's attack,

Also to learn his rank and riches now ;

But Dennell burned with hot surprise and wrath,

And openly, disdaining any word

Upon his station, poverty, or wealth,

Struck at the centre of his right and claim :

" Think you that justice has no part in this ?

" Or that betrothal has no sacredness ?

" If Helen bids me go, I go, nor plead

" A counter-word : but in default of that,

" How shall her father sever us to-day,

" Whose union he approved ? and in this wise ?

" Not by conviction or persuasion urged

" Upon his daughter, but by sidelong stroke,

" Because it chances I am ignorant

" Where now she dwells ?   What method call you this ?

" Unjust and crooked.   Have I injured him ?

" Or has his daughter minished any way

" Her duty towards him these four years, wherein

" Our plighted faith has stood, unmarred by doubt ?

" In patience we abide ; we ask no more——"

But John Dundas broke in with emphasis :

" How know you Helen is at one with you ?

' Four years, you say, your plighted faith has stood ;

" It well may be, she thinks the hoped-for end
" Is proved a failure, and her father's will
" Commends itself unto her wiser eyes.
" A maiden's fancy bends in subtle ways ;
" Up to a time she may have held with you,
" But now no longer."

      Dennell answering cried,
" You err, indeed ! you know not, as I know,
" Your brother's daughter. But suppose it thus,
" As you affirm ; then Helen must resign
" Our mutual bond with that same openness
" With which she gave consent. Procure me this,
" Her own hand's sign to what you urge on me,
" Silent I go ; no more than this I ask ;
" My just demand no plea can countervail."
Then John Dundas a little mused ; at last
(Still following Dennell's lead) he thus replied .
" What hinders Helen, or enchains her hand,
" If she accounts your bond inviolate,
" From sending token of her constancy ?
" You err, in making that request of me,
" Or of my brother, which herself should grant ;
" If you receive not written word from her,
" You must conclude, her mind is changed to you ;
" Perchance she doubts, and knows not how to judge
" Upon the course she has pursued till now :
" Who shall disturb her ? not myself at least,
" Nor one that seeks her welfare."

        Dennell rose ;
A tremor through him ran ; he could not rest ;

He felt a something traitorous, subtly bent
To work his overthrow ; at last with nerves
Strained to their height, he spoke : " My stand is ta'en
" Clearly and simply.   She believed me dead ;
"So ran the tale ; she wrote believing it :
" I ask the proof, she knows me living still."
Then first was John Dundas perplexed in aught.
A sudden memory struck him at that word ;
For noting Helen's sad and wistful look
On that last morning, while she bade farewell,
With some light cheering word he rallied her ;
Whereto she answered, she was glad, not grieved,
To leave her home ; and strange he thought it then :
But sign so dim convinced not ; yet he paused,
Gathering his thought before he spoke again.
" In my poor judgment, 'tis a fair request ;
" Only the answer rests not with myself.
" Write to my brother ; he will satisfy
" Your just desire, and send you true reply."
But Dennell said, " That will not satisfy.
" For say, your brother gives his word that Helen
" Knows me alive, has all an end with this ?
" A hundred chances may have foiled her will ;
" As, the miscarriage of a letter sent
" By her to me ; and she may wait e'en now
" My answer ; or some other idle tale
" Harms me.   Her written word, and this alone,
" Will banish chance, bringing the calm of truth."
With half a smile the other made reply,
" In love and war all chances must be borne."

The youth replied, " There spoke an enemy.

" 'Tis your intent that I should suffer all

" The ills that chance may bring.　Has not your brother

" Each chance already on his side—respect

" Due to a father, old authority,

" Perpetual nearness, choice of time for speech ?

" And must you load the dice with secrecy ?

" I say, if Helen did not love me still,

" You would be prompt to urge her writing now

" To undeceive me.　But she loves indeed ;

" 'Tis proved by this, that you restrain her hand.

" Ay, and I think a thought I ne'er believed

" Until this minute ; for I held till now

" That chance had borne astray the lines I wrote

" From my sick-bed to Helen ; now I see

" That chance was nothing but your brother's will :

" He willed not she should know the truth of me,

" And so with fraud has kept the letter back.

" What say you ? know you aught of such a thing ? "

So Dennell spoke in anger, hitting half

And missing half the truth (as oft is found) ;

For John Dundas was conscience-clear in this.

With paler face, more resolute, he spoke :

" What say you ? that a letter has been kept

" By fraud away ?　That is a word indeed

" That may commend you to my confidence !

" You keep your idle fancies well employed ;

" Yet plainly will I say, it is not true.

" I pray you, take some other theme than this."

And Dennell felt his speech had pressed too far ;

And a reaction set in him once more,
Untwining wrathful thoughts.   " Forgive," he said,
" If I have wronged your brother, or yourself."
Now would he fain explore the true intent
Of Helen's father toward him, and he called
The words to mind that John Dundas had said—
" Entrust a letter to my hand, and this
" Shall duly reach, and duly win reply,"
And was resolving thus ; but John Dundas
Forewent him ere he spoke.   " Young man," he said,
" This matter is but little known to me.
" My brother's judgment I accept herein ;
" Make your appeal to him ; he needs must guard
" His daughter's good ; and if she promised you,
" Long time ago, her hand, it must be held
" Such promise had conditions, limits, bounds ;
" What since has happened was not then foreseen.
" Write, then ; and if my counsel you will hear,
" Be not o'erstubborn in the claim you urge."
So Dennell, though perplexed and much in doubt,
Sat down and wrote, and half compelled himself
To trust in Helen's father.   All his state
He told, and how, by God's good providence,
He 'scaped the triple peril, fire and wound
And fever ; and his new prosperity
Through Conway's help ; and how his present lot
Was bright in promise.   Was it wholly vain
To think that Helen with himself some day
Might yet be joined ? at least, if she herself
Resigned such hope, his right was plain, to know

From her own hand the truth.   And this the more
He must desire, because report had reached
Her ears that he was dead, which till this hour
Perchance she credited.   And then he told
How from sick-bed he wrote to Helen erst ;
But certainly the letter missed, or else
She would have answered.   " I entreat you, then,"
He added, " set within her hand these lines,
"Which to herself I write "—therewith he took
A sheet unmarked ; then thus with flowing pen—
" Helen, a letter from my hand has erred ;
" This shall not err, I trust.   Let one short line
" Say that you know me living ; this as well,
" How you regard me at the present hour.
"If of my state you care to ask, the whole
" Is to your father known."

      So John Dundas
Received what Dennell gave, and promised speed
In sending ; then with questions pertinent
Plied him, and learnt concerning Dennell's state
Much that already had been told with pen,
The same, yet not the same ; for John Dundas
(Being a man high-placed and rich and proud)
Beheld the fact with cool dry vision, stripped
Of hope's bright halo and the glow of youth.
And sending Dennell's lines, he added this—
" Seeing his brother had requested him
" To give report ; the youth was apt and quick,
" By something pleasing charactered as well ;
" In manner ardent, passionate, and filled

"With keen suspicion; one who might in time
" Advance in wealth, not overhigh as yet.
" E'en if he rose, a serious risk would lie
" For any maiden who should graft her life
" Into a land so far and rude and wild;
" Nor could he learn that Dennell hoped to cast
" His lot in England afterward.   In fine,
" His brother was sole judge; but Helen's will
" Might claim respect, and 'twas desirable
" Dennell should be relieved of every doubt."

Dundas in Paris, in his chamber, sat.
Letters were brought; he took them in his hand;
Then laid them on his table, marked them not.
For now his crucial turn of fate was near;
His ripening plans must bloom or wither now;
And fear was chief.   It was the fateful day,
When, as a light cloud rising from the west,
Soon to o'erspread the sky with gathering night
Of tempests, lightnings, thunders, floods outpoured,
The first faint sign of coming war was felt
All through the quivering land; when princes knew,
Yet would not know, the stroke of vengeance nigh.
By the light shadow of that imminent doom
Dundas was stricken; for his proud design
Weighed as a straw in balance 'gainst the need
Of mightier action to the eyes of those
High chiefs of France.   He heard the slighting word,
Which under pretext of delay was fraught
With true repulse, which, were it now confirmed,

Well knew he, France would foster him no more.
For not of those was he who raised the song
Of triumph while the crash of war delayed
And arms were bloodless still; too keen his eye
To be deluded by the films of hope
Which smiling courtiers through vain fancy saw,
Rainbow-like images unreal; he knew
That now or never must he be upraised
To honour by that monarch's favouring eye.
He strove, as if for very life, to bring
His high invention into fields of war,
Till ten days ran their course; then ceased.   That hour
In bitterness he sat, and groaning spoke :
" Undone ! cast out ! as sailors cast away
" The meanest part of all their freight before
" The whirlwind fall ; the boiling surge has scared
" Their timid pulses; had they well perceived,
" I had been worth their saving in this hour.
" Poor fools ! and lightly mocking in their folly
" The wiser-hearted !   What was 't now, the youth
" That hangs attendance on the court, who erst
" Had that soft fawning air, called me to-day ?
" Wizened astrologer.   Well, I can cast
" Their horoscope, and prophesy their doom.
" Ah, and my own ?   Alas ! I fall, and fall.
" Then first ill fortune came, when soft words led
" My spirit to ill-placed trust ; and wealth, that should
" Have grown to double, to a zero fell.
" The height of intellect is maimed for lack
" Of instruments, and men have hearts of sheep.

" What will befall me ?   What shall be my name
" Hereafter ?   Some more fortune-blessed shall win
" This prize of mine—this wonder, this bright torch
" To all the ages.   But in after-days,
" Amidst a crowd of musty manuscripts,
" My own will come to light ; some learned man
" Will read, and cry, Behold ! Dundas foreknew
" These marvels long ago.   O barren fruit,
" Like dead sea apples ! dust rewarding dust !—
" Dennell, false friend ; injurious hypocrite !
" Ah ! would I could be freed from thought of him !
"His son——" He stayed his lips, and broke the
        trance
Of meditation that had brought a sting.
Then cast his eyes upon the table, strewn
With letters ; in their midst, conspicuous now,
His brother's ; for before it had been hid.
Opening, he glanced within ; with sudden start
He flung it down, but now attentive read
With smile sardonic.   " Tender, precious youth !
" So, he would take my Helen o'er the sea ?
" O no, not yet ; he will allow delay.
" I thank him truly.   What says brother John ?
" ' A serious risk ; ' ay, brother, true.   ' Not high
" ' In wealth ; ' ay, true again.   ' But apt and quick ;
" ' By something pleasing charactered.'   Well, well,
" His sire's offence has wiped his merit out,
" Else would I owe him somewhat.   Ah, but now !
" I will not, no I will not, yield to him.
" The ancient wrong endures, and he must pay

" His measure out ; and if it were not so,
" How should I give my daughter up to one
" Exiled in barbarous lands ? How should I fare, '
" Deprived of her, who is my stay, my help ?
" I know these lovesick youths ; they promise much,
" But in the issue will not bear a rein !
" So is it needful to resist at first,
" Nor give that inch which quickly grows an ell.
" And Helen, would she follow him ? who knows ?
" I will not lay the weight of choice on her.
" She has been cold of late. So, he is filled
" With keen suspicion ? How to answer him ?
" Would I could say that Helen knows the truth,
" How he was saved, and knowing breathes in peace !
" Stay——" a remembrance struck him, and he paused.
There was a morning when the public sheet
(The same that erst had told of Dennell's death)
Gave, in few words, reversal of that tale.
Helen, the breakfast ended, must depart
Unto her father's tasks ; and yet the space
Of just a moment she took up the sheet,
And glanced at it, and laid it down again,
Having no leisure nor much care those days
For public matters. Afterwards Dundas
Perused the whole ; then gave it to the flames.
Recalling this, his thought paced swiftly on :
" If Helen knows not, is the fault not hers ?
" I'll not accuse her of such fault." Therewith
He took the pen, and sharpened like a sword
His eager purpose, lest resolve should change ;

Then flinging word on word in scorn he wrote,
As horse that gallops o'er a plain :

      " Dear sir,
" We much rejoice, my daughter and myself,
" To know you have escaped that dangerous mine,
" And your sad illness which ensued upon
" That fiery conflagration.   'Tis indeed
" Matter for thankfulness !   The tidings reached
" Our ears before you wrote.   'Tis also cause
" For much congratulation that it seems
" You now have won a post that will suffice
" To give you sustenance through life ; unless
" You rise still higher, which may happen well.
" I much rejoice, believe me, heartily.
" Now for that other matter, whereupon
" Your letter seems to call for some reply.
" 'Twas but a foolish business ; but at length,
" Frankly I tell you, it must have an end ;
" And truly glad am I to see that now
" You make appeal to me as one whose voice
" Can judge in this your suit.   My answering word
" Cannot be doubtful ; though a youthful mind
" May deem it hard, yet is it salutary :
" Dismiss the thought, which hinders you so much,
" Of wedding with my daughter ; circumstance
" Has set a bar, which cannot be removed.
" Why, when my daughter, as yourself confess,
" Replied not to your letter sent before,
" Urge you again ?   Persistence does her wrong.
" Is then a maiden ne'er allowed to rest

" Who once has lent her ear to love's fond tale ?
" What would you ?   Must I use authority,
" And make her answer you ?   That cannot be ;
" For since your father's sad untoward acts
" It was against my will she wrote at all.
" Neither is any need, herself should write ;
" For, for the substance of the thing you ask,
" Myself can answer quite as well as she.
" Take then as final this, which now I send.
" She has at length in fulness recognized
" Her duty towards her father, cheerfully
" Acknowledges my judgment as the best
" That can direct her, and has acquiesced
" (And without pang, if I am not deceived)
" In thinking of yourself as one whose lot
" Cannot be joined in any way to hers.
" From your own words, if you recall them right,
" You will perceive you have no claim on her
" Henceforward.   So, I pray you, cease to strive
" To mar her duty and our happiness ;
" And I do hope you will be soon content
" With some esteemed companion, who will share
" Your joys and sorrows in that far-off land.
" My daughter sends her kind remembrances,
" Whereto I add my own."

      So much he wrote ;
And boldly superscribed the city's name,
Paris ; he liked not aught that seemed to hint
Concealment ; also he must shortly leave :
Then sealed the letter, saying to himself,

" If aught in that should chance to be untrue,
" At least the whole may very well be true,
" Excepting Helen's kind remembrances ;
" And that is a mere form, as all agree."
Then once again : " The Scripture says, the sins
" Of fathers fall upon the children's heads.
" So it is now.   And have I not the right
" To guard my daughter from her foolishness ? "

Though many cry,
What sin it is to lie,
Yet they who bear
Truth's travail-pang, how rare !
Twofold the pain
Of him who would attain
The land of light :
To clear the clouded sight,
And fashion struggling speech in words that aim aright.

If thou through tears
And toil and trembling fears
Hast found the clue
That severs false and true,
Yet, yet beware !
For through the teeming air
(Out of the deep
Wherein thy passions sleep)
Storm-clouds may rise and break, and spoil what thou
wouldst reap ;

And wilt thou then,
When all is known to men,
Blameless appear,
In every part sincere ?
Scarce will it be,
  . If snares have compassed thee.
Strive only this,
To atone where thou didst miss ;
And trust that dark shall yield to light, and sorrow's
touch to bliss.

Dennell, two days ere Conway's suit must close,
Received the lines of subtle guile and scorn
Writ by Dundas.   What anger filled his veins !
His bosom heaved, he panted, utterance failed ;
Abruptly then into his sister's hand
He thrust the lines, his sister Mary, she
The confidant, through this last month, of hopes,
Conflict, and fears ; and crying " Read ! " he rose
And left the room.   She read, and followed him ;
And placed her arms about his neck, and soothed,
Until his passion worked itself to calm,
And then he spoke.   " What lying spirit moves,
" Mary, in men, I never knew till now.
" My God ! it is a monstrous lie, to say
" That Helen without pang abandons me.
" I say, she knows not yet I am alive."
And Mary answered, holding still his hand,

". Truly my grief in this your grief is great."
He keenly looked at her. " Believe you, then,
" What I have said ? " She answered, " I am slow ;
" I have no skill to judge ; it may be true."
" It may be true ! " he cried ; " 'tis true, indeed."
Again his sister : " I would say a thing,
" Only I fear." " What thing is this ? " he said.
" You are too troubled and too passion-wrought
" To-day to judge the lines of false and true."
" I shall not change to-morrow from to-day,"
He answered, " No, nor any day to come,
" Till Helen with her lips reveals the truth."
" Why should she have aught more to tell than this,
" That she has yielded to her father's will ? "
" If she had yielded to her father's will,
" She would have written, ay, with her own hand."
" She may have yielded," Mary said, " in part ;
" She will not write and wholly break your bond ;
" She dare not write and say she keeps it whole."
" So would not Helen ; she had dared the truth.
" And after I was lost, wounded, and sick,
" Accounted dead, and then past hope restored !
" She to keep silence ! never would she so.
" O Heavens ! and see the message he pretends—
" Her kind remembrances ! 'Tis false as hell ;
" Those words ne'er came from Helen."

                                        " Say 'tis so,"
Said Mary, " yet it follows not that all
" Is a mere fable. It is natural
" She should have yielded. There must come a time,

" When every man, and woman too, is weak.
" When she believed you dead, 'tis probable
" She on her father leant, more than before,
" And made some promise she could not take back
" After discovery of the truth ; indeed,
" 'Tis even possible she wrote to you,
" Her father knowing nothing, and some chance
" Carried astray the letter on the road."
" If it be so," said Dennell, " 'tis the same.
" Something is lost between us ; whatsoe'er
" That something be, I'll seek and find it yet."
" Seek then, and try to come to speech with her,"
Said Mary ; " letters will not profit now.
" I read the matter thus : her father's will
" Has been too strong, is tyrant over her ;
" That he is hard, and full of wrath and hate,
" Stands plain.   I hate him in good truth myself.
" The fox ! to hide himself, nor let you win
" A glimpse of Helen.   But I gather this,
" That Helen loves you, will not give you up ;
" Else had she written surely.   Tell me now,
" What were your aim, if you had speech of Helen ?
" Is it that she should brave her father's wrath,
" And follow you ? for if in last resort
" She willed not this, your search were little use."

Then Dennell mused, and answered, " I had ne'er
" Thought of the end ; I was too full of wrath.
" But, Mary, what you say is truth ; Dundas
" Has thrown a challenge in my face, and I

" Take it ; 'tis open war, I will not spare.
" And being present, I shall have command
" Over her spirit ; ah, what have I said ?
" Command her spirit ! she it is till now
" That has commanded mine ! Well, be it so ;
" I love her still. But if 'twere true, the thing
" Dundas has boasted ; if she flung away
" With a light smile my heart, how were it then ?
" But that is false ; he lies. Yet if in aught,
" Why not in all ? Is this not false, that Helen
" Knows I am living ? Mary, judge and say."

She answered : " Has he lied before to-day ?
" Or know you aught to give a vantage-ground
" For such a charge ? "
               He paused, but spoke at last :
" I could not say it. I remember now,
" That when in furious rage he flung reproach
" Against my father's honour, and I stormed
" Indignant at his slander, he was moved
" To make withdrawal of the lying phrase,
" Though arrogant beyond all limit still.
" I could not say he did it as a man
" Dishonourable by nature. Be it so.
" I go to Paris. Mary, you will join
" With me in search ? "
               " Ay surely," she replied,
With cheerier voice, " and courage ! I have hope.

Now Conway's suit was crowned with happy end.

O

And Dennell heard the favouring word, the seal
Of justice that approved his cause, and so
Was gladdened; but far more because his feet
Were free at last to move in dearer quest.

He had been told of some, as ancient friends
To Helen's father.   Two alone had seen
Dundas in London, when the waning year
Threw over street and square his foggy shroud;
And unto one Dundas had named his goal,
Paris.   At that confirming word the heart
Of Dennell leapt.   With Mary o'er the wave
He passed; and lo, the city, fair and proud,
But trembling with expectance fierce and keen;
For war's dread dice were cast; the end was hid.
Brother and sister heard the hum of men,
The tramping legions' stir; and who could choose
But pause and listen to that mighty sound,
Though passion in him flamed?
                                   Upon the day
When August wakened, bright with sunny glow.
They found the home that held of late Dundas
And Helen; but it held not now.   'Twas said
That they had sought the Tuscan city, throned
By Arno's waters, whence the royal sway
Stretched over Italy, though soon to find
More venerable seat.   So Dennell went
Thither; but Mary stayed behind, and sought
For any that had met in daily life
Father and daughter, and had known their mind.

And Dennell dwelt in Florence, in the house
Whereto Dundas should come ; sure proof was seen
That this was so ; among the letters set
Conspicuous on the wall for future guests,
Some for Dundas, and one for Helen, lay.
And when a week had passed, a letter came
From Mary, left in Paris.   Thus it ran :
" Dear brother, there is one who holds command
" In that great army marching now for war
" Eastward, who often with Dundas was joined
" In converse grave and long—Carrère his name.
" His wife I saw, who said their common theme
" Was something of wide import in the realm
" Of science ; more than this she could not say.
" But this, alas ! she added, when I asked
" Of Helen : how she was most dutiful
" And faithful toward her father, and in toil
" Incessant, which confirms in part his word ;
" Nor any sign of strife 'twixt him and her
" Could I elicit.   Rather, when the wife
" Once questioned Helen, ' Wherefore think you not
" ' Of marriage ? ' Helen answered, ' See you not
" ' My father's matters on my hands are laid ? '
" But never of yourself said any word.
" Yet was she sad and pale.   Now, it may be,
" Brother, I err through ignorance ; for ne'er
" I met with Helen, never word or sign
" Between us passed ; but may she not have held
" More lightly by your bond than you have deemed ?
" And is it well to waste your days too much

" In sorrow ?   Pardon me ; perchance you know
" More certainly, and more to your content,
" Than I."

But Dennell wrote in answer thus :
" Not lightly Helen did maintain our bond.
" Yourself shall read the words she wrote to me,
" Then judge.—I have no certain news to tell.
" They must come hither ; letters wait them here.
" But if they come not ere the month be past,
" Then must I sail for Rio.   Therefore write,
" Mary, with your own hand to Helen now ;
" And with your hand address it in her name,
" But send it here to me ; and when I leave,
" If still she have not come, it shall be set
" In faithful hands ; it cannot miss her then.
" Say you desire that she herself should write ;
" That she is free to bring our troth to end ;
" No thought of anger in my breast shall dwell.
" Only, until herself has written this,
" I am much troubled ; for I fear to take
" Another's witness in so dear a thing ;
" Her own assurance, though it bring me grief,
" Will bring me peace.   To me she need not write ;
" To you it will be better."

Mary read,
And wrote to Helen.   Thus the letter ran :
" Helen Dundas, I ask a simple thing.
" If it be true, as truly I believe,
" That through your father you have signified
" Your wish to make of none effect the troth

" Betwixt my brother and yourself, then write
" This from yourself, and sign and send it me.
" My brother has no angry thought of you,
" But is much troubled ; for he fears to take
" Assurance from another ; your own word
" Will give him grief, 'tis true, but peace as well."
Further, the sister to her brother wrote :
" My father needs me ; homeward I depart."

And Dennell stayed until the month had past ;
Then leaving Florence, where his hope had grown
High as a flame just ere the last collapse,
Placed Mary's letter in the hand of him
To whom pertained the house and all its care ;
And spoke : " The maiden named, as here you see,
" Will shortly come ; then give her this ; take heed,
" No other hand receives it save her own.
" But if she come not ere September's close,
" Then send me word ; forget not ; I would give
" Large recompense to any man who told
" Where now the maiden and her father live."
The other promised due and faithful care ;
But Dennell with a heavy heart returned
To London.   There in sadness, yet at rest,
He spent two days ; then stepped aboard the ship
That southward sailed across the Atlantic deep.
Again the mountain-girdled bay, again
The city, chief of all Brazilian realms,
Received him.   Conway praised his toil, his zeal ;
And in reward of these assigned a share

Of independent right, as unto one
Subordinate no longer, but conjoined,
And next to Conway in his wide affairs.

'Tis harder, when the dreams of youth
Await in hope the seal of truth,
To watch them dwindle day by day
In dubious, lingering, slow decay,
Than when Fate's sword, descending sheer,
Smites off their blossoms clean and clear.

Yet thou, whose trembling thoughts aspire
To some fair image of desire,
Be not (howe'er thou pine forlorn)
O'erquick to cast away in scorn
Visions, that under cloudy skies
Have shone to thee like Paradise.

For if thou hold thee patient still,
Sincere in love and strong in will,
The day shall come that parts indeed
Mirage from truth and flower from weed;
Whose issues, whatsoe'er they be,
With light and peace shall comfort thee

Though twice a thousand leagues of land and wave
Divided from her lover's waking eyne
The fair sad face of Helen ; though a sire
By craft had cut the thread that bound those hearts
Together ; still had they been joined anew,
If Chance had spared his blow.
                                        For when Dundas
(At bursting of the thundercloud of war)
Had ta'en departure, Helen at his side,
From Paris ; first his purpose was, to seek
The Tuscan city ; then the weariness
In Helen's eyes, her fevered restlessness,
Turned him aside ; and in that Paradise,
Where Alpine snows o'erhang the flowery vales
Of Italy, he deemed she would revive.
But Helen's soul and body, deeply hurt,
Though hiding pain, refused the remedy ;
She saw, but could not feel ; the secret foe
Gathered, and in Verona brought her down
Nigh unto death.   Then was Dundas assailed
With bitter thoughts ; for if ambition ruled
Paramount in his heart, his daughter's weal
Was after this most dear ; nor e'er before
Had she been sick, who feared not mist or storm
On Cumbrian hills, or toil of hand or foot
From girlhood's opening hour ; and could it be
That she should sink, she die, so full of life ?
Not for a moment had he feared such ill ;
Yet now upon the sharp precipitous edge,
From whence one little touch would send her o'er,

She lay.   But he that tended her with arts
Of medicine, marked her fevered cry, which told
How far she wandered through the maze of dream,
Answering to voices heard by none beside ;
He asked, if any sorrow burdened her.
Dundas with sharp disquiet turned away ;
" I know not," he replied, but knew full well ;
And that same day he sought the aid of one,
A kindly Englishwoman known of old,
Loving, and loved by, Helen ; and she came ;
And Helen by those gentle ministerings
Was won to life, and felt the touch of love
Cherishing all her weakness, and awoke
To conscious sense ; and presently she poured
The pining current of her inward grief
Into the ears that heard her tenderly ;
Weak as a babe, she uttered all her soul.
The father heard it ; he revolved his sin ;
And in that balancing 'twixt life and death
Which held his child for doubtful days and nights,
Almost was minded to undo the past,
And speak the word restoring ancient joy.
Only, his deeds would shame him, brought to light ;
This held him back.
                    But while he mourned and feared,
A sudden summons bade him come with speed
To Florence ; one in power desired to learn
His secret art.   He journeyed, and three days
Dwelt in the city, basked in courtly smiles ;
Yet to the end, in solid recompense,

Knew not if he had profited at all.
The fourth day dawned ; he hastened to depart ;
Then did the master of the house draw near
(Mindful of Dennell's charge) and questioned thus :
"Return you hither? will your favour light
"On my poor house again? and she, who now
"Tarries behind with sickness, will she come
"Some day to Florence?" "Ay," Dundas replied,
"Your friendly roof shall shelter us, be sure,
"When once my daughter is restored to health."
Full well the master bore in memory
How Dennell straitly charged him not to give
The letter unto any other hand
Save Helen's only ; and the word was sure,
Promising she should come ; he deemed it best
Not yet to yield his trust, but hold it still.
Also Dundas had promised this with truth ;
With truth of heart ; the issue went not so.
For as he journeyed back, his purpose changed
Through unforeseen event.   Upon the road
He met a keen, impetuous soul, by race
Italian, living on the southern heights
That look o'er Florence to Fiesole ;
To whom he presently imparted much,
Through gradual converse, of his great design :
The other, fired with new ambition, urged
Dundas to rest beneath his roof, a guest,
Whene'er he came to Tuscan soil again.
Which so ensued, and thither afterwards
Father and daughter came ; it happened thus

That Helen ne'er set foot within the walls
Where Mary's letter lay awaiting her.
Such was the blow that marred the final hope
Of Dennell.   Ah ! not will with will alone
Must strive, but with this blind material frame,
Whose lifeless substance hems and straitens in
The flood of life.

              From Florence, o'er the crest
Of Apennine, to where Bologna shows
Her slanting towers, and thence across the plain
Spanned by the northern river's placid wave,
Dundas returned; and now Verona's walls
Were won; "Thy daughter lives," 'twas answered him.
He entered in, and saw her pale and thin,
But softly breathing.   Truly Helen's soul
No less than body had been cheered and healed;
Full of all comfort was that gentle nurse;
And Helen hoped contentment might be hers,
If but her father would resume the look
He wore to her in childhood.   And behold,
He stood beside her suddenly; she marked
The lines of care and pain upon his brow;
Was it for her?   He came, and softly spoke:
"Daughter, 'twas told me thou wert sick at heart
"For matters past.   Now tell me truth, I pray,
"If wasting grief possesses thee this hour."
She smiled: "'Tis true, I have been overworn;
"But fear not, for the peril is o'erpast:
"Be not o'ergrieved yourself; it were not well."
"It is a heavenly frame, my child," he said;

And forth he went and spoke within himself;
"Too late it is for change; for good, for ill,
"The thing that I have done is done and o'er.
"Is then the common word, that all things come
"To light at last, a truth?   If so it be,
"All men have something hidden, and my share
"Is like the rest.   The roots of things are fed
"In darkness; darkness to myself has been
"Needful herein : let come what will; enough."

Helen arose from sickness, and then came
To Florence.   Often did she love to seek
The peaceful aisles that breathe divine repose;
There pain grew mild; the silent airs were balm.
But as she gathered strength the glory fell
Upon her spirit of that land, the gem
Of all earth's beauty; ancient ages stirred
A wondrous power and mingled with her blood;
For by the mighty signs of Night and Day
That breathe in marble the universal pang
Of man's and nature's travail, and the rest
That closes labour, fashioned by the hand
Of Michael Angelo, she loved to sit;
By this and by all grace of outward things,
Which in the very stones of Italy
Has a true being : and by the genial air
And the blue sky and mountain peaks far seen
From San Miniato 'gainst the setting sun,
Her heart received a solemn tender joy :
Again she wrote to friends; 'twas hard before;

For grief endures not talk of trivial things,
Which meet the eye but to the soul are dumb.
But now high souls were mixed with hers, and made
Her words the veil of deeper things within,
Which else the cold air had to silence chilled.

But all in vain, beside fair Rio's bay,
Dennell awaited sign from Helen's hand.
Howbeit the faithful host, the Florentine,
Fulfilled his promise, when September changed
Into the misty month of falling leaves,
And wrote to Dennell; Dennell learnt this way
How Helen at Verona had been left
Through sickness, but would surely visit yet
The Tuscan city, when her health returned,
And sojourn in that hospitable home.
So much he learnt, but afterwards no more;
The Florentine wrote once again, but knew
Nothing of Helen, nor had seen Dundas
A second time; and deep the trouble lay
In Dennell still.
              But Mary had been sought
In marriage, and became a bride, a wife;
And coming once to Westmoreland, she asked
Concerning Helen: but could hear no word.

When from the east the cold clear day was born,
    Far o'er the fruitful level plain arose
High peaks ethereal, crowned with golden morn,
    And raimented in strength of stainless snows.

But as I journeyed on, the lesser hills
　　Came in between and hid that heavenly sight ;
And then in cliffs and woods and falling rills
　　And spaces of green lawn I took delight ;

And when the noon grew hot in heaven, I lay
　　In shade of elms with chestnuts intertwined ;
And children heaped on me in laughing play
　　The fallen flowers, and ran and looked behind.

And then there came a maiden, young and fair ;
　　Ah me, how fair ! and in her eyes there gleamed
A light more clear than sunrise, and her hair
　　Down to her feet in golden masses streamed ;

Her gentle voice, her timid trustful look,
　　With musical soft love were overflowing :
She led me past the fountains of the brook
　　To caverns cool, with fern and mosses growing,

And fed me with soft words, nor e'er withdrew
　　Her hand from mine, her eyes from off mine eyes ;
My heart beat fast ; nor whence she came I knew,
　　From earth, or flood, or depth of azure skies.

Ah, whither is she fled ?   I did not weep ;
　　A flash, a cry ; then fell my fainting sight.
And afterwards I wakened, as from sleep,
　　And saw the earth, and men, and heaven's fair light.

Upon Ferrara's head a price was set;
Denounced by speech and writing through the land,
In darkest dens he lurked; the toils were drawn
Closer; and now he called to mind Peranne,
And sought the house where dwelt companionless
That ardent gentle spirit; 'twas the night,
And falling rain and thunder. Truth to say,
Peranne was bent at last to leave the land,
Where all his toil for Sylvia had been vain;
But not as yet his thought had grown to act.
Thin, haggard as a ghost, with eyes that flashed
From hollow cheeks, Ferrara entered in;
Then spoke: "O sir, your mind is just and kind;
"The men of blood pursue me; shelter me
"This night alone; to-morrow sails the ship
"To bear me far from this accursèd land.
"You once partook with me my humble fare.
"Oh, I am saved, if you deny me not!"
A spear went through Peranne, and touched a nerve
Which needs must answer such appeal from one
Who, like himself, was wrecked and desolate;
"A dark recess is close above," he cried,
"Hidden by faggots; there conceal yourself."
Ferrara upward clomb; and now Peranne
Began to think, and murmured: "Am I then
"Complicit in all acts, whate'er of guilt
"Ferrara has essayed, or secret war?
"Well, it is done; I trust the better chance."
The morning came, eight strokes by chiming clocks
Were sounded; and Peranne had carried food

With his own hands to where Ferrara lay,
But quietly was seated in his room ;
Hark ! a loud knocking 'gainst the door beneath ;
With pomp and noise the officers of law
Swarmed through the house.   It was not long, and lo !
Ferrara manacled was downward brought ;
And he that seemed in chief authority
With clanking sword and martial gesture strode
Into the room where sat Peranne (for this
Was first explored, and still a guard was there),
And cried : " 'Tis needful that you follow me.
" It cannot be without your aid that one,
" A villain sought so long, that he may pay
" Just penalty for horrid murderous deeds,
" Lay hidden here.   And see, he has been fed ;
" To harbour such an one is treasonous crime."
Peranne replied, " Conduct me as you will."
Along the streets Ferrara and Peranne
Were led together.

               Dennell had returned,
Three days before, from Europe ; in that hour
To Conway's office he was speeding on ;
He saw the prisoners, and a jeering crowd ;
Then recognized Peranne.   With wonder filled
He crossed the street, and spoke : " What dismal sight !
" What is the cause, Peranne ? and can I aid
" Your freedom ? "   " If you will," Peranne replied,
" My deepest thanks are yours ; I have no friend,
" And need one truly."   'Twas the noonday hour
When Dennell found Peranne in prison cell.

" Say, of what charge you stand arraigned ? " he asked.

" For having sheltered that conspirator,
" Who waged a secret war against the state."

" Ferrara ? " Dennell questioned.   " Ay, the same."

Then Dennell, smitten with keen pangs for her
Whom he had lost, cried out : " Ferrara ! he !
" By heavens, the injury I bear through him
" Defies all speech !   You sheltered him, you say ;
" Were you his friend ? or knew you not the man ? "
With frowning brow, and gesture stern and harsh,
Thus Dennell spoke ; far other was his mind
Than when, the year before, he had conversed
With Conway and with Sylvia ; but Peranne,
Feeling the hostile mien and words, replied,
" Your prelude argues, you would not be found
" My advocate ; go hence, if so you will."
And Dennell left the cell ; but ere he reached
The prison gates, he wavered, and once more
Entered and spoke : " I would not leave you thus,
" Except with clearest proof.   But this I say :
" If you were hand in glove with that vile crew,
" Aided or sanctioned that conspiracy,
" Your help must come from others, not from me."

" I never joined their deed," replied Peranne.

" How came it, then, Ferrara sought your aid ?
" Why gave you aid, and sheltered him from law ? "

" For pity's sake, since he was desolate ;
" And I had known him in the years gone by ;
" When, I deny it not, I also knew
" Something of his intents ; but joined them not."

But Dennell cried, "Such knowledge is too much
" For perfect unsuspicious innocence.
" Methinks you were his sympathizing friend ;
" Looked on his villainies with tender eye.
" Dare you affirm, this moment, that his deeds
" Deserve not punishment ? "

       Peranne, at this,
Sighing replied : " Alas, and must I stand
" As judge of others, in these strifes of men ?
" Is't not enough to answer for myself ?
" Yet this I say, and truly I can say it,
" Whate'er by word of reason I could urge
" Against these deeds which you term villainies
" (And rightly, it may be, you term them so),
" That did I urge ; not knowing more, indeed,
" Than this, that something of a violent sort
" Was in the mind of these conspirators ;
" But knowing that, I strongly did dissuade
" Such course ; nor saw them afterwards at all—
" Save twice, I think, Ferrara greeted me
" At turning of the road, and I replied—
" Until that hour when he implored my aid
" (Yesterday, suddenly, in dusk of night)
" Under my roof."

      Then Dennell paused ; at last,

" More than discouragement," he said, " is due
" From one who knows the framing of a crime.
" Were there not those who would have stayed its course,
" Guardians of public weal ?   What held your tongue
" From warning these,—a plain, clear remedy ? "

" I knew not any point," Peranne replied,
" At which their purpose aimed ; nor any man,
" Saving Ferrara ; all the chiefs were veiled,
" When once I saw their nightly conference."

" Natheless some general word was in your power.
" Also one point at least you knew exact—
" Ferrara's name."
                        Peranne, so much assailed,
Grew hot, and cried : " Before I answer you,
" I pray you tell me, is it friend or judge
" I see before me ?   If a friend indeed,
" Ask not that every tittle of my acts
" Shall be a flawless diamond in your eyes ;
" I joined Ferrara for one cause alone,
" Seeing we held, the people suffered wrong
" Through law and custom ; afterwards he erred ;
" Which, when I knew, I went with him no more ;
" Dissuaded much : what more require you, then ?
" Call you it duty, to betray the man
" Who trusted me, had broken bread with me ?
" What you have suffered hence, I know no more
" Than what myself may suffer ; but 'tis truth,
" There is no single act that I have done

" Which had for aim, or as I think did tend
" To these untoward lamentable deeds ;
" Which sprang from sickness through the hearts of men
" Throbbing, beyond my power to staunch or cure."

And Dennell now was softened, and he said :
" I came not here to mock you, but to aid.
" I will revolve the matter in my mind,
" And speak again ere sets to-morrow's sun."

Dennell that evening supped in Conway's house,
And told Peranne's misfortune in a tone
Of interest blent with pity.   Conway spoke
Severe reply : " The man of whom you speak
" Is under grave suspicion, and I fear
" Justly : his life has lain in doubtful ways.
" Make then inquiry, ere you aid his cause."
Clara and Sylvia sat and held their peace.
And Conway afterwards to Dennell's ear
Disclosed the life Peranne was deemed to lead :
" Howbeit I know not ; Hardiman affirmed
" 'Twas mere eccentric humour ; yet take heed
" Ere acting further."   Dennell once again
Was dubious ; and his work was pressing then ;
Half was he minded to dismiss Peranne
From thought, unholpen.   Thrice the night grew dark ;
Peranne, unvisited, well-nigh despaired.
But on the fourth day's afternoon it chanced
That Dennell came to Conway's house again
In search of something lost ; and Sylvia marked

His entrance from the garden, where she sat.
He issued forth; she met and greeted him;
Then quickly, and in firm, emphatic tone :
" Believe not what was told you of Peranne.
" Ask and discover.   He was kind to me
" On board our vessel ; 'tis my debt to him,
" To ask your kindly service in his cause.
" He is an Englishman, in peril here,
" Perchance of life ; you will befriend him, then ? "
Dennell was conscience-stricken, and beheld
Her manner, piercing and imperative ;
" I will befriend him," he replied ; and she,
Saying, " 'Twill not repent you," touched his hand,
And moved away, more stately than her wont.

So Dennell made inquiry, wheresoe'er
Peranne was known, of converse, manner, life.
And last, he sought Ferrara ; who appeared
Proud in demeanour, scorning bonds and death,
But sketched Peranne in plain and truthful phrase,
As one of strenuous simplicity,
Honest, unwary, whom the world's fine snares
Would surely make to stumble.   Dennell heard,
And took his way to Conway's house at eve ;
There spoke conviction, how Peranne's offence
Was not of deep irreparable stain,
Nor with dishonour mixed in any guise.

So with what help was needful for a man
Charged with deep treason and conspiracy,

Peranne was furnished; and the cause was heard:
Ferrara, glorying in his crime, foretold
Revenge; but presently in milder tone
Declared the innocence of him who stood
Arraigned in fellowship of bonds with him.
But justice held not so; and judgment went
'Gainst either head, though not alike the doom;
For on Ferrara sentence was of death,
But for Peranne a year's imprisonment.
And this he counted light who knew at last
Conway appeased, and Sylvia friend again;
For Dennell so declared.   And Dennell bore
Unto Ferrara from Peranne a word
Before his hour of death.
                              But when the year
Was past, Peranne, departing o'er the deep,
Saw lessening, fading on the horizon's verge,
That shore, the scene to him of love and pain.
A northern clime by Massachusetts bay
He sought, and that famed city; there he deemed
Were men and ways most suited to his mind.

Have patience, O my soul, nor seek to know
    Whether the work thou workest shall abide.
    All mortal things must first with fire be tried;
And some must fail, and some have bitter woe.
Dismiss vain longings, steel thyself to bear,
And having purposed strongly, strongly dare.

"Ah, surely," say'st thou, "though my work decay,
    "Yet shall the height of my intent be known
    "And honoured among men when I am gone ; "
What noble spirits have been reft away
From earth forgotten, leaving not a sign
Of pains and struggles far exceeding thine !

Or say'st thou haply, "There is laid in heaven,
    "For those who toil and suffer, great reward."
    Think not of that ; whatever there is stored,
Is not as wage at stated season given,
But by his word who from the central deep
Assigns just lot to all to smile or weep.

When thou art wafted through death's gloomy strait
    Unto the land of righteous doom or praise,
    There shalt thou find thy friends of other days ;
But shall they stand with thee in equal fate ?
Or how if they with lustrous deeds shall glow,
While thou, abashed, hast nought of worth to show ?

"Ah, pure immortal spirits," thou wilt say,
    "I am not worthy ye to me should speak :
    "Yet look upon me, tempest-tost and weak."
And they in love will look on thee that day,
But not for long, for they have tasks to do
In mightier regions far beyond thy view :

Faint not that hour, but cleave unto the root
    That nurtures all eternally ; from thence

Strong life shall come and flow through nerve and
    sense ;
It may be thou wilt yet bear worthy fruit ;
And then those others shall with thee rejoice,
And thou wilt hear the music of their voice.

———

Briefly had Dennell, when he reached Brazil,
Told Conway of his failure and distress
Concerning Helen.   Then the older man
Pitied, but could no more ; till growing months
Gave shape and colour to a dawning thought.
For, noting Dennell with a watchful eye,
He deemed his fire was lessened.   " Ill it were,"
He thought, " if disappointment chilled the blood
" Of one so brave, through some deluding chase."
So pondering, he discerned at last an end
Commendable and worthy, that should cure
Both Dennell's, and another's, restlessness.

Sylvia of old, though liking Dennell well,
Had felt him irresponsive to her touch ;
For part the maiden left on English shore,
And part his work constrained him ; and a mind
Preoccupied bends not to any call ;
But that companionship in perilous hour
Beneath the burning rafters of the mine,
And afterwards, when hardly saved he lay,
Bereft of sense and motion, on the brink

Of th' awful smoking gulf, her hands the while
Laving his wounded brow and round his head
Binding her own soft kerchief—this had made
A friendlier sense between them ; and the more
When by her lips he had been moved to shield
Peranne from danger.   So they slowly grew
In knowledge of each other ; and the thought
Had glanced on Conway once or twice if these
Should wed each other ; but the fancy passed ;
Till one day made it firmer.
                              Sylvia's tone
Had gathered nerve and strength, but varied still ;
For mostly with a cheerful readiness
She gave obedience now, and lent her ears
To Clara's words, and uncomplainingly
Moved in the common round.   And when the day
Declined to eve, before her father's feet
She sat, and would caress and stroke his hand,
Greeting him with soft nothings as he came
From desk and office, seeking rest in shade
Of flowery alleys, or on balcony
That looked o'er bay and mountain ; and he loved
To hear her talk upon the world's affairs,
Which much engaged her fancy ; so the weeks
And months passed on, but not for ever so ;
For presently 'twas seen a spirit worked
Within her, and o'erflowed, and would not stay
Within its straining confine.   Suddenly
(After long days in meek retirement passed)
She would arise, what time the darkening sky,

Cloven with lightnings, showed the coming storm,
And seek the thunder-echoing crags, and there
Endure long time, and dripping wet return
With eyes that glowed ; and nothing ailed her thence ;
The inner fire sustained her.   Or from morn
She left her home till evening ; whither gone,
Herself confessed not, but 'twas said she rowed
Her skiff among the bays and fairy isles,
Which are the jewels of that inland sea ;
And whether she had talk with fishermen
Or with no mortal creature but the winds
And waves and whispering forests, none could tell.
And Clara felt that Sylvia would not brook
Control, and in such seasons held her peace ;
But Conway was perturbed, and feared some ill,
When once he knew it ; gently he reproved :
But Sylvia scarcely answered.   Yet she soothed
Her father with obedience afterwards,
In quietness performing all his will,
Until the passion rose again in her.
One night, her father being away from home,
She in her skiff lay all the silent hours
Watching the stars ; returned at last at dawn
Dismayed was Clara ; Conway heard next day ;
And as it chanced, Dennell had come with him,
And underneath the shadowing boughs they two
Went on, and Sylvia met them on the path ;
And Conway sharply chid the maiden now,
Saying, she ne'er must wander so again ;
But she with pleading softness answered him :

"There was no danger, father ; truly friends
"More than you deem are mine ; and such were nigh
"Last night within my reach, if I had need.
"The myrtles overshadowed me ; the sea
"Lapped on the rocks, and lulled was every wind.
"Yet pardon my offence ; indeed I erred ;
"I will not roam so long, unknown to you,
"Henceforward." Conway was but half appeased ;
"Have I not cause for anger ? " he exclaimed,
Turning to Dennell. Dennell answering smiled :
"Nay, she has spoken fairly ; she is brave,
"And yet she yields ; and can you ask for more ? "
"I thank you, friend ; your words are ever kind,"
Said Sylvia then. And Conway marked the words
And cordial look of either. From that hour
He strove to join them in the marriage bond.
"Dennell has lost for ever," so he thought,
"The maid he sought ; he needs a steadying aim ;
"And Sylvia's volatile and wilful soul
"Through worthy converse will grow strong and calm."
But Conway named not to himself Peranne
(Who now three months had left Brazilian shores),
Nor cared to think of him as one whose lot
Had been entwined with Sylvia's.
                              After this
Did Conway once or twice, half-conscious, hint
Something that much perplexed the younger man.
One day it chanced that Dennell sat alone
In Conway's house, upon the balcony ;
Unwonted was the fashion of his thought,

Soft melancholy musing :
     " Woods and hills,
" Rills of the vale, and murmuring ocean flood !
" Why is it ye, unasked, unrecompensed,
" Lay out your sweetness for our hearts' delight,
" Who are so distant from your race ; while men,
" Our kindred, stand aloof, and aid us not
" In all our pinings ? but ev'n ye, I deem,
" Mountain and glen and ocean, wore of old
" A kindlier look ! " Now Sylvia came behind,
And wondered, seeing him so deep in thought,
Yet roused him not, but silent went her way.
Next came her father ; with the second sound
Dennell awoke, and Conway thus began :
" Ah, and had Sylvia aught to say to you ? "
Then after pause (for Dennell answered not) ;
" A pretty fortune will be hers some day,
" My girl's, when I am laid beneath the ground."
He tarried not ; but with the word a light
Flashed upon Dennell ; " Conway wills that I
" Should wed his daughter ; " perturbation deep
Filled him, and anger, and he hastened thence,
And shunned the house awhile. In course of days
He wrote to Mary, told of Conway's hint ;
The sister answered, she must needs rejoice
In such an issue ; Dennell was displeased,
Reading her answer.
      Sylvia, too, was stirred
Through Clara in these days. For Conway's wish,
Imparted to the elder dame, had won

Her staid approval ; and her cue was ta'en
Gently to sound the ways of Sylvia's heart.
And after trial indirect, she deemed
Explicit word might pass.   One day they came
Together from the city ; Clara then :
" Lies there aught adverse in your mind to one,
" Sylvia, who has been known to us long time,
" And long esteemed,—who did companion you
" In deadly peril once, and saved you then,—
" Whom afterwards you helped to save in turn—
" To Henry Dennell ? "   Sylvia, wondering, cried,
" Nay, wherefore ? he was ever friend to me."
" It has been in your father's mind and mine,"
Clara pursued, " how good an end it were,
" Should he and you agree in mutual troth,
" And afterwards be wedded in due time."
But Sylvia cried, " O what is this you say ?
" Cease, speak of it no more."   But Clara said,
" I would not wound you, Sylvia ; 'twas indeed
" Your father bade me ask you."   Sylvia then :
' Has Henry Dennell spoken aught of this ? "
And Clara answered, " Nay, I know no word.
" But what your father has observed, or knows,
" May be of greater import ; many things
" In silence find expression.   But 'tis meet,
" Though Dennell ne'er was named by us at all,
" That you should have a serious thought of life."
And thus beginning, Clara gently swerved
To themes more general.   When they reached the
    house,

They parted from each other ; Sylvia strayed
Along the garden, through the wicket gate,
Down to the beach with mighty boulders strewn,
And leant on one, and thought of days gone by,
And listened to the gently rippling wave,
And watched the line of sunset glory stream
Across the sea.   An hour she lingered there.

———

How oft, in decay of some dearest affection,
　　When far from the crowd the lone spirit has fled,
O Nature, thy balm o'er each sad recollection
　　And desolate fancy has gently been shed ;
How oft were we soothed by the clear running river ;
　　The hills in their glory, how raised they our soul !
Life breathed in the glade where the forest leaves quiver,
　　And power in the ocean's long thundering rolL

Ah, can it e'er be, thou wilt change to our feeling ?
　　Shall all thy bright scenes but remind us of pain ?
Shall mortal embitter thy fountain of healing,
　　And peace on thy breast shall we look for in vain ?
What shadows are these with the woodland that mingle ?
　　Our loved ones of old, whom we cherish no more !
And the sunlight is chilled over torrent and dingle,
　　And our eyes fill with tears by the surf-beaten shore.

O heart that of man and of nature art weary !
　　Why linger, when all thy frail courses are run ?

Since here is no love and no beauty to cheer thee,
  Confess thee deluded, despairing, undone.
Nay rather, O dawn of the world's renovation,
  Rekindle our torches that flicker and die,
And flush with the freshness of primal creation
  The eye and the ear and the earth and the sky !

The day drew near, when passion's battling powers
Must strive for Dennell's soul.   His thought of Helen,
Devoid of outward food, must slowly yield ;
'Twas as a citadel, still standing safe,
Though outworks crumble one by one, and fall.
And be it said, that Conway's, Clara's words
Had wrought in Dennell and in Sylvia thus,
That neither could with frank unconsciousness
Receive the other's glance ; and each would fear
That something dwelt within the other's soul
Unguessed, unwished.   Through chance the crisis
    came.

Two years had fled, the third half-way in course,
Since Dennell left the soil of Italy :
One day it came to pass, he entertained
Comrades in Rio ; Conway, he alone
In elder years, among them ; all the rest
Were youths, from divers countries and remote
Gathered ; but Valdez, native of the soil.

And after talk and circling wine and mirth
That merrier grew, a stripling rose and filled
Brimful his glass—tall, glancing-eyed was he,
In gesture bold; from Michigan he came;
He spoke that all might hear: " Our company
" Misses the fairer counterpart of men;
" Pledge we the absent, naming each the name
" Of her he deems most fair."   The rest acclaimed;
Careless, impassioned, serious or in jest,
They toasted each the maiden of his choice,
Or whom he feigned his choice; some lingered on
Half-willing, and a casual converse rose;
And Dennell's turn was last; he thought, perchance,
He should keep silence even yet, nor name
Her, whom to name was pleasure on his lips;
But Valdez now was challenged to a song,
Who with a cheerful welcome thus replied:

O friends that with jubilant motion
    Of youthful adventurous blood
Have sought o'er the wild rolling ocean
    Our region of forest and flood;

Since none but myself of your number
    Awoke to the fire of our clime
From softness of infantine slumber,
    I weave you a welcome in rhyme;

While changeful the seasons are fleeting,
    May your fair ones be changeless and true;

May their bright eyes grow brighter in greeting
   The fame of the deeds ye shall do !

What island or continent holds you
   Hereafter soever, I pray,
Forget not the land that enfolds you
   With smiles of her sunlight to-day ;

And think from afar on the singer
   Who seizes the hour in its flight,
And woos the sweet echo to linger
   In chambers of breathing delight.

But stay ! for a name must be spoken
   By our comrade, our host, and our friend ;
Come, Dennell, delay not the token !
   What toast is reserved for the end ?

All looked on Dennell, while he rose and spoke ;
" Once did I know a maiden passing fair ;
" This to her memory, to a vanished form—
" Helen ! "   He drained the glass, and set it down.
And Conway heard, and thought, " The hour is come ; "
And framed his full intent.   Next day he spoke
To Sylvia, setting forth his tenderness
For her, his child ; and of that future time
When she of him protectionless must go
Through the world's perils ; also it were well
If she should marry, though he would not dare
To press her wishes ; yet he longed to know

She was not careless of her future life.
And Sylvia with affection answered him ;
" She was not careless : but her thoughts indeed
" Were hard to utter ; they escaped herself."
Then Conway asked her pardon, while he named
The name of Dennell.   Sylvia answered him,
" O father, Clara spoke to me erewhile
" Of that same thing ; and I could scarce reply
" With calmness ; for such thought had been in me
" Never ; 'twas pain ; and wherefore should I frame
" Imaginings that could not grow to fruit
" Save through another, who had made no sign ? "
And Conway said, " Nay, if it gives you pain,
" We will not speak of it.   But all can see
" That Dennell much regards you.   'Tis enough
" What I have said ; but have I hurt you now? "
And Sylvia answered, " Nay, you hurt me not."
That evening Sylvia asked, if ever yet
Peranne had written from the northern land.
Her father answered, none had heard of him ;
And Sylvia felt a blankness in her heart.

Like to a tree that in the opening year
Buds with a gradual growth, now shooting out
This side, now that ; so Conway's purpose grew ;
And leaving Sylvia, he to Dennell turned :
One day he asked, if tidings yet had come
Of Helen ; Dennell answered, no : again,
" Your hope remains ? " then briefly Dennell spoke,
" A plant in barren soil unwatered pines."

'Twas not long after, Conway plainly said,
" If you would marry Sylvia, many a doubt
" Would find solution, many a pang be lulled."
But Dennell started, for the voice struck through
Right to the very centre of his soul,
As if a vision that he fain would bar
Was now with force insistent ; and he turned
In anger, crying, " You are strangely wrong.
" Helen is in my thoughts, Helen alone ;
" I have no satisfaction in my heart
" Concerning her ; how can I think of aught
" In way of marriage, while this hangs in doubt ? "
" What ask you, then, to satisfy your heart ? "
Conway replied ; and Dennell spoke again .
" Two months in Europe, there to find or miss."
Conway, astonished at the answer, paused ;
But soon recovered breath, and said, " 'Tis yours."
Dennell was silent, in his turn amazed ;
Such swift acceptance seemed beyond belief ;
Neither was Conway's air as one of thanks
Expectant ; in brief words agreement passed,
Almost as if with awe on either side.
In April, Dennell sailed the second time,
With other temper far than such as raised,
Three years before, his swiftly beating heart
In glad impatience o'er the tossing waves.

Father and sister he rejoiced again
Beholding ; she no more a maiden now,
But newly married ; and she longed to see

Her brother happy, even as herself;
But doubted how to speak to him, nor knew
Why he had come across the deep again.
At last she dared to say, "You told me once
"Of Sylvia Conway; I would gladly hear
"Further; for I was pleased you wrote of her."
But Dennell answered shortly, "'Tis not she;
"Helen Dundas is in my thoughts to-day."
Brother and sister knew discordance then
Within their mutual hearts, and said no more.

Then Dennell came to Westmoreland, and asked
Of Helen in her village; and he spoke
To many there; for folk remembered him.
With him they mourned for Helen.   Dennell saw
The ancient gardener who had served Dundas;
He in his cottage garden plied the hoe,
And said, "We looked, sir, you should marry her;"
Then fell to work again; but Dennell sighed.
"Letters," the gardener said, "have come from her;
"But 'tis a year ago."   And Dennell learnt
But little more from any, saving this,
That Helen was in Florence, twelve months since.
Tarrying a week, to Mary he returned;
Who cried, "It grieves me, brother; for I bring
"Tidings, but not good tidings.   One who dwelt
"Last summer through in Florence, tells me this;
"That Helen with her father lived retired;
"He was a man mysterious and reserved,
"Nourishing some deep secret; Helen's look

" Was fair but melancholy ; it was said
" That she should marry, ere the year was out,
" A gentleman of Lombardy, by name
" Ridolfi.   And my friend believes it true."
Dennell, brief questions and replies exchanged,
Kept silence.   Afterwards he learnt that one,
Known to Dundas in London, had received
A letter in the waning of the year ;
Dundas from Venice wrote, but asked reply
To Dresden ; Helen was not named by him.
Dennell to Florence journeyed, gathered there
For certain, that Dundas with Helen left
The Tuscan city, ere November's close :
Ridolfi was remembered, and was known
To be with sire and daughter intimate,
But left the city earlier by a month
Than their departure.   Dennell, little skilled
In the Italian tongue, was forced at last
To recognize defeat ; nor more availed
His quest in Dresden.   Musing by himself
An hour alone, conclusion sad but clear
He made ; that Helen in all likelihood
Was now a wife, and surely should no more
By him be seen.   To England he returned.

So Dennell closed the memory of his past ;
Bankrupt of hope, yet shielded from despair.
Soon came the backward voyage.   More content
Than he had e'er believed were possible,
He saw the shore of England fade behind.

And when he came to Rio, that same day
He told the whole to Conway, who returned
Brief answer, not unfeeling ; nor a word
Concerning Sylvia.   None the less a shade
Different from heretofore in Conway's tone
Was felt by Dennell from that hour ; as though
A tacit claim were in it, not severe,
Reserved, and blended with a kind regard.
And Dennell yielded, for of sympathy
Great was his need, ay, and of something more.
For thus he thought : " My life's first act is past.
" Youth's passion will not come a second time.
" Alas ! my inward glory is all gone.
" How shall I clothe these tender thoughts, that long
" Have been my portion and my very self,
" From the rude air ?   Enough :—I must not think
" Of what is possible."   But after that
He oftener went to Conway's house, and found
From him a ready welcome, ever kind.
·But Sylvia looked perturbed.   It came to pass,
One evening, after Dennell had gone o'er
In thought his years of life, all that had been,
And what was now, and what should be to come,
He looked at Sylvia ; she upraised her head ;
Directly thus and suddenly they gazed
Each on the other ; each received the strong
Unquailing glance ; and then they turned away.

Sylvia.

O stars of piercing might,
   To you, through silence deep
And breathings of the night,
   I lonely weep;

And ask if you have seen
   With your pure eyes intense
That faithless I have been
   To innocence;

Or wherefore lies the load
   So chill my heart upon?
The stern and joyless road
   Still lengthens on.

Ah, whither is he fled
   Who walked with me of old?
Perchance among the dead
   Entombed and cold!

Did I repel him, then,
   When love was once so near?
Will he not come again
   My heart to cheer?

O heavenly pardonings,
   Whate'er my fault has been,
Unseal your sacred springs
   And cleanse my sin;

Dissolve this icy chain ;
O let my spirit's sigh
Be breathed in generous pain,
Or let me die !

Peranne in Boston found it rather gain
Than detriment, that he had suffered bonds
In Rio for political offence ;
Also from England friends commended him ;
And snares were none ; a sudden favouring stream
Bore him along, who in a narrow nook
By reeds and rushes had been prisoned erst ;
He prospered, and with growing weal.   And now
Little expected friends were found hard by,
Farquhar, and Laura ; he, the stalwart man,
Though slow of brain, had won prosperity.
With these Peranne grew intimate, and more
And more each day ; and Laura's sympathies
Were of the tenderest ; and so at last
He told concerning Sylvia, and his hope
Some future day would bring accomplishment
Of all that dream or vision, night or day,
Had whispered of love's fair reality.
And Laura asked him once, if ever he
Had seen or heard of Sylvia since the day
When all his woes began ? and he replied,
That on the day before he left Brazil,
While he was standing on an open ground

Beside the bay, and many to and fro
Passed, or for pleasure's sake reclined and gazed
On the far mountains and the sparkling sea,
Sylvia was riding by her father's side
A little space below ; he saw her there,
And would have slightly swerved another way,
But she glanced upward, and with gentle curve
Made her steed turn, and rode to where he stood,
And asked him how he fared, and on what day
He sailed, and hoped that they should hear of him.
He answered, how he knew not ; and she joined
Her father ; who from distance gave brief nod,
Scarce looking back to see Peranne's response.

And after this, it happened there was need
That Farquhar should to Rio sail once more
For final settling of engagements made
In years gone by ; and Laura, though her wont
Was ever to abide at home for sake
Of children three that had been born to them,
Accompanied his voyage, for some cause
Disclosed to none ; but, ere they left the land,
Peranne, with much entreaty in his look,
And more in word, to Laura came and asked
That she should take a letter in her charge ;
" Say what is best, and all you know of me ;
" And give this too, unless you know 'twill move
" Sylvia against me."   " Surely," Laura said,
" The letter shall be given ; and I will say
" All good of you."   Next morning they embarked,

And reached the southern city thirty days
Later than Dennell's second sad return.

———

O'er the hills a-maying,
'Mid the blossoms playing,
Strayed a boy and girl in days of old ;
Love, like summer lightning,
Through the twilight brightening,
Like a secret thread of gleaming gold.

Hark, what horsehoofs prancing !
See, what spears are glancing !
Foemen ride and tear the girl away ;
Love in that fierce hour
Flashed with mighty power,
Kindled into flame his deathless ray.

She, all lonely fretting,
Home and kin forgetting,
Far removed beside an alien wave,
Still through pulses tender
Saw her dear defender
Imaged as he stood, in act to save.

He in dreams the sighing
Of his child-love crying,
" Come, O dearest playmate ! " heard, and wept ;
So in manhood's budding
(Courage through him flooding)
Girt he on the sword, while others slept.

Many a stormy water
Traversing he sought her,
Many a woodland wild and haunted land;
Till he saw the maiden
Gazing, sorrow-laden,
Seaward from the solitary strand.

Then, her dear name sighing,
She with his replying,
Through their eyes the springs of love were found;
Passionate that finding,
Ne'er unloosed the binding
Which they knit upon that sacred ground.

CANTO V.

THE VOYAGE OF HELEN.

Was Helen wedded wife indeed? Not so;
Though with entreaty wooed, and strongly urged.

Not long her father and herself abode
Within the house that sheltered them at first
In Florence. He, the friend and host, that gave
Promise of partnership in that high aim
Wherein Dundas was toiling, must depart
Far from the Tuscan city; he was made
Heir to estates far off, that long had lacked
The hand that should control them. Now, at last,
Dundas began to feel the dreaded sign
Of inward change; he was not as of old.
His soul's unrest turned to his body's bane.
Shaken he seemed, as if some nerve were torn
Too vital to be healed; upon his brow
Fear was inscribed, and trembling on his lip;
Yet lacked he neither industry nor thought
Nor painful application; in the root
And central being he was marred and worn.
A weary man, he sought the ear of kings;
The vestibules of great ones of the earth
Knew him too well; how many an hour he conned
Persuasive speech, and fence of proof, and seeds

Of reason, which on barren rock or brier
Fell ever, but not once on that good ground
Which gives the giver back an hundredfold ;
Or if some heedful mind took note, and seemed
On point to yield, that show deluded still ;
Hope dwindled more ; from shock to shock he fell.
How different from those early days, when he
In his ancestral home with patience probed
Nature's great secrets ; when ambition ran
In peaceful currents, undisturbed by haste ;
When passing hours were joyous, and a glow,
Caught from the future, lighted up new worlds
Like far-off mountains in the sun's last ray
Gleaming ; but now no more with genial warmth,
Rather an icy blast from spectral peaks
Pierced to the bone, 'gainst which no cloak could shield.

And Helen seeing this was wrought again
To pity and to love him ; and she placed
Her service like a mantle round his need ;
And thought no more of all that she had deemed
Unkind, unjust ; but lightened with her talk
His frequent gloom and sad despondency.
Also she shared, as in the past, his toil.
And while the second summer sped its course,
There came the suitor that was named ; for he,
Ridolfi, was by kinship near allied
To him their sometime host ; and oft he saw
Helen, and marked her filial care, and heard
Her converse wiser than her years, and felt

Her gentle grace, and so was moved to love ;
To him Dundas gave welcome, and of him
Would speak to many ; and the rumour grew
That surely Helen was betrothed to him.
Which was not so ; but Helen held him still
In disapproval, and for righteous cause ;
It needs not now to tell such tale in full.
But evermore Dundas would think, " Hereby
" My daughter shall be sheltered when my head
" Is laid in dust ; " and foolishly he deemed
Her true and ancient lover's loss no more
By her should be lamented.   Yet he learned
Through time the truth, that Helen would not change ;
Likewise Ridolfi learned, and came no more.
And after this the soil of Italy
Grew to Dundas each day more wearisome.
November came ; and with the waning year
A promise from the German land was brought ;
"Come, Helen, come," he cried ; " we yet will win
"New life, new fortune, in a happier clime."
O'er Apennine and Alp they went, and passed
The city, Austria's crown, where Danube rolls
His breadth of waters ; and in Dresden's walls
(Of German cities friendliest and most fair)
Tarried (for rest was needful) some short space ;
Thence to the new-made empire's seat of state
In Prussia's plain ; there dwelt the winter through.
But with the spring a languor took Dundas ;
And Helen feared ; for neither seemed he now
Apt for life's fray, nor yet content to yield

His part therein to others ; strain and care
Harried his spirit, sleep forsook his eyes.
Sickness at last, and weariness long drawn,
And gentle suasion of his daughter's voice,
O'ercame his struggling will ; and sad at heart
They left the busy city's throng, and sought
A quiet hamlet on the lonely shore
Beside the murmurs of the Baltic wave.

HELEN.

O gentle wind, that breathest o'er the sea
    Upon the swelling buds of spring,
      And passing tremblingly
    The loving birds that pair and sing,
      Reachest to me, ev'n me,
Filling my heart with memories and sighs,
      With tears mine eyes,
    How is it that thou canst not bring
    The spirit of my youth again,
So long forgotten, and now sought in vain ?
      The fountains of my grief
I know ; but those of succour and relief
Escape my very soul's imagining.

The summer came—the fourth since Helen left
Her English home ; the little hamlet still

Beheld her, on the margin of the sea
Whose inland waters from the German coast
Roll unto Lapland.　All the sunlit hours
She sat, and watched her father.　Sick he lay ;
Wearily did he move his hand, and breathe
With heavy breath, and all his strength was gone.
And Helen knew the end was surely nigh.
A pang o'ercame her ; now her heart presaged
The days to come—how desolate of all
Her feet would move from land to land, and find
No home where'er they wandered ; or perchance
A sharer in the world's gay busy round
She would be seen, yet meet no kindly eye,
And hear no voice that thrilled her soul to hear ;
Or if returning she should seek again
Her native village 'mid the hills she loved,
How would all things be changed, e'en those that
　　seemed
Changeless ; and how should she endure to climb
Where once she clomb, or sit beside the brook,
Lonely, and listening to its merry song ;
How see the garden where her lover last
Had parted from her eyes, ere yet he sailed
On that sad voyage which had been, she thought,
To him the passage to the land of death ;
Yea, e'en that garden now no more was hers ;
All things were reft away.　She sighed ; but saw
Her father wakening, hastened to his side.
Uneasily he strove to rise, but sank
Backward, and whispered, " Helen, I shall die."

She took his hands in hers, and knelt, and wept,
Hiding her face; but he began anew;
" How will you fare, my child, when I am gone ? "
" Father," she answered, " even now it came
" Into my mind ; I was afraid, but yet
" To fear too much were wrong."   " And care you
        not,"
He asked, " to know the wealth that will be yours ? "
" Tell me," she said.   " 'Tis fair, and will suffice
" For more than simple needs ; but yet no voice
" Will call you rich.   Had fortune favoured me,
" It had been otherwise."   " That matters not ;
" Grieve not for this," she answered.   Now he lay
With face averted ; presently he turned ;
" Is marriage in your thoughts at all ? " he asked.
" I have no mind to marry," she replied.
" You will be lonely."   Then again he lay,
And spoke no word ; but spread the coverlet
Over his face, and dozed, or so it seemed.
At last, " It cannot be, you grieve till now
" For that forgotten matter ? " so he asked ;
But she, " For Harry Dennell ?   I have ne'er
" Forgotten him, nor shall."   He answered not ;
And presently she left the room, and went
Unto her chamber.
                        After this, Dundas
Revived for some short space ; and in those days
Helen received a letter from the friend
Who nursed her in her sickness, and therein
Was written, " Dearest Helen, be not now

"Amazed too much, or borne beyond yourself.
"'Twas told me, Henry Dennell lives to-day.
"I can but say the thing I heard; myself
"I needs must doubt it; 'twas affirmed, he 'scaped
"Out of the fire; his sister told the tale
"To one who told it her that told it me.
"But where the sister lives, or if she be
"Maiden or married, this I could not learn."
But Helen, breathless, laid the letter down,
For all her heart was leaping in her breast.
Incredulous she must be; yet she laid
The lines before her father's eye, and cried,
"Can it be possible? it cannot be——"
"What cannot be?" the father drily spoke.
"It cannot be that Henry Dennell lives."
"Why, certainly it cannot be," he said.
Fear made him stony; Helen with a pang
Felt the vain beating of her heart's warm blood
'Gainst this cold barrier.   Now Dundas foreknew
His treacherous act some day would come to light;
He looked upon his child beside him there—
How worthy of a father's tenderness
To foster and to shield! and ah, how soon
In this wide world would she be desolate!
Almost, not quite, he was resolved to say
The truth, and ask her pardon whom he wronged;
And now she took his hand in hers, and cried,
"O, if it should be!   Father, be not hard;"
He could not answer yea or nay, but drew   ·
Gently his hand from hers.   A sudden thought

Came over Helen; " Father, you have ne'er
" Learnt aught of Henry Dennell since the day
" When we together heard that he was slain?"
He could not answer. Flashed through Helen then
Terror, with lights of hope unbearable.
He raised his eyes, and with a sidelong glance
Beheld her trembling ; then at last he spoke ;
" Ay, he is living." " Ah, when heard you so?"
" 'Tis three years since." " O, and you kept it back
" Through all my grief, when I was sick at heart,
" In body too, and near the brink of death !
" How strange, how cruel !" " Well it is," he said,
" To fling reproaches on me, when I lie
" Upon the bed from whence I ne'er shall rise
" A living man again." " O pardon me,"
With tears she cried, " and yet—— " But he pursued ;
" Well is it that you seek to wed the man
" Whose sire was first to pull my fortunes down ;
" Go seek him, wed him ; youth with youth should pair ;
" You will be happy ; leave me here to die."
Now Helen felt injustice in the word,
And won composure back : " Until this day,
" Father, I have with all obedience wrought
" To do your pleasure ; never, while you live,
" Will I forsake you. But I needs must ask,
" First, where is Henry Dennell at this hour—
" If so it be you know; unless, indeed,
" You wish to sunder us for evermore ;
" So harsh you could not be !" A moment's pause
He made, then answered : " I have yet his lines

"In which he wrote where he was living then,
"Among the secret papers in my desk."
Now Helen felt the very truth was near.
"He sought me, then," she said; "how answered you?"
Dundas kept silence longer than before,
But broke it with a firmer voice at last:
"Helen, deep bitterness, and harsh unrest,
"Possessed me in the hour I wrote to him.
"I told him, from obedience to myself
"You had resigned the wish to be his bride."
He backward sank upon his bed; but she
With inarticulate cry rose up and passed
Into her chamber, knelt before her bed,
Burying her face; ah, who shall say what thoughts
Within her surged, what powers upheld her then!
Ne'er did she stir; the summer day went by
From noon to waning light, still knelt she there.
Rising at eventide, she sat awhile
Beside the window, gazing o'er the sea;
Then to her father came, and said no word,
But kissed his forehead. Silent he received
The silent token; presently he slept.
When morning came, she served him as before,
And spoke of many things with tearless eye;
Saying, she would have friends; he must not doubt
She would be happy; and what pleasant sights
And kindly folk they met in every land:
And then she touched on happy childish days,
And how he taught her, wandering o'er the hills,
The names of birds and flowers; and he replied

In softened tone, tho' brief in word, and seemed
In manner grateful.   Once he looked at her
Long time, and held her hand ; and she believed
He asked forgiveness in the speechless act ;
Whereat the fountains of her heart unsealed
Came flowing through her eyes, that were inscribed
With things unutterable ; a deeper breath
He drew, then loosened hold ; but seemed content,
Yet after this his strength, an ebbing tide,
Forsook him daily.   Now he seemed to think
His daughter was a child again, and they
Dwelling in Westmoreland.   But more and more
He slept ; one night he wandered ; and at break
Of day he died ; and Helen closed his eyes.

And when her father had been laid in earth,
And all things duly ordered, Helen came
To England.   Dennell's lines—a fragment torn
Out of the letter—had been found, and told
That Rio was his home three years before ;
The vision grew in her that she must sail
For Rio ; yet she feared.   It was required,
For perfect settlement of all affairs,
That she must seek her uncle, John Dundas.
To Kendal's vale she went ; and when the sum
Of those immediate needs was brought to close,
She spoke upon her deeper need of heart,
Saying, " 'Twixt Henry Dennell and myself
" The troth remains unbroken at this hour."
And John Dundas, recalling Dennell well,

Pitied the maiden, but was fain to check
O'erhasty action.   " Helen," he replied,
" Myself will write to him whom Dennell served,
" The merchant Conway ; he will surely say
" If Dennell prospers.   Rush not hastily
" Into a matter full of chance and doubt ;
" It e'en may be, your lover has despaired,
" And ta'en another bride.   If 'tis not so,
" Then may we hope that all by gradual steps
" Will be restored, to your content and joy."
But Helen answered, " Uncle, this were kind,
" If you should write.   I thank you, but I doubt ;
" For if my heart accused me afterwards
" Of cowardice—— "   She paused at this ; and he
Spared further question on the thing she meant.
Next day she sought the village of her birth :
Her eyes o'erflowed, beholding it afar ;
Each fold of mountain slopes, each scar and stream
And hidden glen, through sight and sound could breathe
A spirit into hers.   And now she drew
Nearer ; the village folk with glad surprise
Welcomed her coming ; he, it chanced, the first,
Whom Dennell met, the gardener.   Ah, what tale
Was this ! how Dennell in that very spot,
Not two months since, had stood ; and how he asked
For Helen, saying there was pressing need
That he should find her (breathless Helen heard) ;
And that his time in England was not long—
That for Brazil he must depart again.
Others confirmed the word, and added more.

But Helen hastened to a secret place,
O'erpowered.   She must conceal from every eye
The deep emotion that possessed her then ;
For they that saw her wondered at her look.
Upon the grass, where witnesses were none
Save flowers and birds and trees and falling brooks,
She flung herself and sobbed ; for joy and fear
By turns came o'er her ; all the images
Of years gone by began to shape themselves
Into one living current, and impelled
Her soul to energy.   At last she rose ;
Returned to Kendal, to her uncle's house ;
Next day to London journeyed, and inquired
From one whose name she called to mind, as known
To Dennell's father, where the son might be.
Who answered, he would seek to learn.   Through him
Did Helen learn, that twenty days before
Dennell had ta'en departure for the lands
Across the southern ocean.

                         Now indeed
She might not tarry, since himself had said
The need was pressing ; resolution came,
Strong and unshakeable—herself must sail
Thither, where he had gone.   But John Dundas
Perturbed in heart, and fearing grievous ills,
Hastened to London, and dissuaded much,
Saying, she was embarking on a course
Daring and perilous, that well might bring
Reproach upon her ; he himself would write
To Rio, asking more of Dennell's state ;

So were a prosperous end most surely won.
But Helen with entreaty and with tears
Answered, the need was great; and she would keep
Her purpose secret, saving from the ear
Of him, whoe'er it was, that held command
Of Henry Dennell's service ; so should none
Esteem her overbold.   At length she won
Her will, so pleading; and the uncle sought
Through his acquaintance some one who should know
Conway, or any that in Rio dwelt :
Helen, where'er he went, accompanied.
It was not long ere one was found, who said,
" I know not Rio of myself, but there
" My brother and my brother's wife have dwelt
" Five years ; and surely they will help you well."
He paused, and looked at Helen's tender grace ;
Then added : " Gladly, lady, will they take
" Yourself beneath their roof ;" with brief delay,
Demur, and thanks, conclusion so was made.
So, preparation ended, on the ship
She stood ; the furrowing keel began to cleave
In westward course the foam ; a solemn calm
Upheld her ; all her thoughts were borne afar
To where this grosser earth takes fire from heaven,
Warm with the glow of hope.   At close of eve
Standing beside the prow she murmured thus :

" O happy night ! O blissful time ! O waves
" That dash your spray afar against the verge
" Where lingers yet the buried sun's last glow !

"O take me, bear me thither ! surely there
"Within those golden vaporous halls dark-hung
"The quick ethereal spirits live and breathe,
"Nor alway are disjoined from us, but pierce
"With their pure flame this bodily garb, and pour
"Their voiceless music on the living soul.
"O come, if there ye be, and lead me on
"Safe in these paths, where all unskilled I go :
"For never felt I as I feel this hour ;
"And yet my feet in childish days have pressed
"Full many a sunlit spot, and answering love
"Has shone to welcome me ; but now the world
"Spreads far beyond my ken ; th' illuming ray
"Kindles the depth before me, and I see
"The forms that mingle with our life, and lead
"Our mortal being to its goal. Ah, yet
"May no fond fancy cheat me ! for no more
"Can I control th' unbidden thoughts that come,
"But needs must follow to their hidden end."

She came to Rio ; 'twas the second morn
Since Farquhar had with Laura touched the land.
Ere noon the friendly house was found, to which
She was commended. There was she received
With honour ; for a something in her air
Had grown, which told a purpose in her heart
Stronger than woman's wont ; yet strong with love.
At eventide she needed some brief pause
Of silence, so to gather up her thought.
Upon a path retired she took her way ;
The sunlight was upon her as she mused.

Now flaming hearts aspire
Up to the starry fire,
    Winged for a flight unending
With throbbings of desire;
But 'tis, alas, in vain;
When they the goal would gain
    No longer sweetly blending,
    Dissevered and contending
They fall to earth again.

O maiden innocent,
Whom thine own soul's intent
    With courage has persuaded
And for deliverance sent;
Canst thou the snares divine
That round thee subtly twine,
    Or vanquish all unaided
    The foes that have invaded
The peace of thee and thine?

*   *   *   *

What did I hear in a dream?
A sound of galloping feet,
A sound of coursers fleet;
But they and their riders were hidden, apart from the
        morning's beam;
Darkness upon them lay,
But yet mine inner sight
Was lit with sudden light,
Whereby I knew that they

Dominion held, and bore
To mortals evermore
The keys of fate;
And is it for bliss they are come, or is it too late, too
late?

Dennell with Sylvia went at eventide
(For in her father's garden meeting her,
He made request that she would come with him)
Along a path, that from the city led
And wound along the hills above the bay;
And in a little glade, receding thence,
They sat among the trees. The path hard by
Lay in their view a few yards' length, no more,
This way and that screened by the dell's steep bank;
Beyond, the sea shone bright; the hills behind
Rose in their steepness. Then a silence came,
And Dennell thought within himself: " The hour
"Is come to act. Decision has been ta'en;
"Ay, it was in me, while I yet did pause,
"And think that I was taking counsel still.
"What now can come from heaven, or earth, or hell,
"To stay the word that fate compels and sets
"Upon the lips that shrank from utterance
"So long—and would they find a respite still?
"It shall be." " Sylvia, be my wife," he said.
"Yes, be it so," she answered; and she laid
One hand on his, but with the other made
A guard to hide her eyes, that filled with tears.

But he looked over her, and saw the path,
And saw the sunlight streaming on the sea.

It was the hour when Helen set her feet
To seek the lonelier hilly ways, that so
She might in silence muse and ponder o'er
Her meditated act ; a tender fear
Blent with her heart's pulsation, and her lips
Trembled, and yet her eyes were steadfastly
Set on the far clear heavens, as if she longed
That all her purpose should be sifted through
By some diviner judgment ; on her cheek
The hue of youth glowed deeper than was wont ;
Upon her forehead and her flowing hair
The light fell golden :—
                    Lo ! as Dennell looked,
She who was ever in his thoughts went by.
A moment, and her presence pierced him through ;
Up from his seat he rose, but felt the hand
Of Sylvia ; ah, his eyes are fixed ; 'tis she,
'Tis she indeed ! how could he fail to know
Each radiant feature, loved in years gone by ?
For time nor grief had dimmed them, nor availed
To write hard characters on that soft brow,
Nor dulled that fire, nor sullied that pure calm :
Looking straight onward, quietly she walked ;
And if her form seemed different in aught
From that which in the vales of Westmoreland
Had been the centre of all images
Within his soul (how deep engraven there !),

It was but in her statelier mien, that grew
From deep endurance and high thought ; and now,
E'en as she vanished, on her wrist he spied
A silver bracelet gleaming, his own gift,
With serpent's head and curious chasing wrought ;
He gave it in that golden summertide
When earth and heaven consented to their troth :—
Panting for breath, upon his breast there lay
A weight that hindered speech ; in vain he strove
To murmur "Helen !"　So she passed ; the place
Was void where she had stood : for fear his blood
Was stayed within its courses, and each limb
Imprisoned motionless : but Sylvia now
Was looking on him.　" Is there aught amiss?
" What have you seen ? " she trembled as she asked ;
For pallor and the dark foreshadowing
Of something nameless had o'erspread his face ;
At last in broken hollow voice he spoke—
" Sylvia, go home and wait."　And saying thus
He from her hand unclasped his own.　She rose,
And with a quivering lip but silver voice
Answered, " You tell me not, my friend, the thought
" That troubles you, or what has come to pass ? "

" Tis nothing—yes, 'tis something ; it may be
" To-morrow I will tell you ; no, indeed,
" I may not promise ; 'twill be in the end
" Nothing : but leave me now."
　　　　　　　　　　" You scorn me, then ? "
" I scorn you not ; leave me ; 'tis but this hour.

" Ah me, what have I said ?   I pray you go."
" If you have any gracious thought at all,
" Send me not from your side until I reach
" My father's door."
                  " The way is safe," he said.
" Is it, then, safer than your company ?
" Is this your trust in me ?   Did I persuade
" That you should lead me hither ?   Was it I
" Who asked that we should join in such a bond
" Wherein our mutual souls might be as one ? "
So Sylvia ; but with vehement accent he
Made answer : " Come !" and led the downward way
With silent speed (yet upward once he glanced,
To see if Helen might be still in view ;
But her a turning of the path concealed) ;
Sylvia with steps unequal followed him.
To Conway's house they came ; then neither spoke ;
She entered in ; but he at racing speed
Ran back and upward.   Soon he passed the spot
Where they had sat ; beyond, a triple way
Diverged.   He called with all his voice and strength,
" Helen !"   An echo answered, twice and thrice
The sound was carried, half he deemed the hills
Were aiding and half mocking ; but reply
Was none ; along one path he went ; and now
Threading the mountain ways, he called to mind
That day long past, when on the Cumbrian hills
He followed her, the maiden yet unknown,
Through bush and glade ; O would she now as then
Smiling return, and chide his skill-less feet ?

Alas! not so; to every road he went,
And where a village crowned the cliff; but none
Had seen her; then returning, at the spot
Where he had sat with Sylvia, he again
Took seat; perchance she might return that way;
"O vision of my soul! O grief! O fate!"
He muttered; then with irony, "This scene,
"Is it not what my heart has pictured oft?
"How she should come before me suddenly,
"Fresh from the ocean ways, the rosy morn
"Colouring her cheek, and laughter in her eye,
"Crying, 'At last I come to thee!' and now
"She is here. What brings her here? Is it for me?
"It cannot be, if she annulled our troth.
"She wore my bracelet; was the marriage ring
"Upon her finger? Would that I had seen!
"Oh, 'tis for me, for me, I know it well,
"She comes; and I will find her—yes, to-night,
"To-night, where'er she be; I cannot fail.
"And then, O happiness! the years of gloom
"Wiped out, or but remembered as the cloud
"Which makes more fair the sunlit earth and sky!
"But what of Sylvia? She has trusted me;
"Nay, but if Helen has preserved her faith,
"The ancient bond stands clear. But is it so?
"I will not think, but find and know the truth.
"The stars are kindled; 'tis too late for her
"To come this way returning. I will go."
He went; and in the city, till deep night,
Explored each place where Helen, as he deemed,

Might pass her sojourn ; yet he found her not :
Neither next morning, when from earliest dawn
He toiled in search, did fortune prove more kind :
Now must he meet with Conway in the ways
Of daily duty ; how to speak with him
On what had passed ? and must he yet preserve
The bond with Sylvia ? 'twould seem the maid
Whom yesterday he wooed had right to learn
His purpose, whether still the same or no ;
But to that seeming right his angry soul
Gave obstinate resistance.   " Nay !" he cried,
" My secret shall not yet be torn from me !
" Does Sylvia suffer wrong ? not mine the hand
" That injures her ; and yet I may have sinned.
" But who can always guide his steps aright
" In misty mazes wandering ?   Yet excuse
" Were vain ; upon my head the punishment
" Will fall, if fall it will ; I cannot now
" Avert it ; by compulsion I am urged
" Upon the path I tread, though all is dark ;
" I scan the tempest-laden air with eyes
" That fain would pierce to the heart, but shrouded lies
" The lightning in its bosom.   O come forth,
" Pierce me, if so it must be ! better far
" The blow once fallen, than that which ambush'd lies,
" Which wearily we look for day by day.
" Or, heavenly powers ! is this my punishment,
" Friendless and lone to chase a phantom fire ?—
" Stay !   It may be, if Helen's father strewed
" Indeed with guileful snares his daughter's path,

S

"And if she have discovered this at last,
"She thinks my ancient post retains me still,
"The mine.   Ay, so it may be ; and the road
"Takes her three days to traverse, barely that ;
"And I will send a trusty messenger
"To question at each point, if she is there,
"Or has been seen ; and if she reach the mine
"Even five days from now, then two days more
"Will give me knowledge of it, ay, or less ;
"A week I must endure, and Sylvia wait,
"If wait she will ; but if she will not so,
"Broken our bond must be."
                              And Dennell sent
A trusty messenger at every point
To ask, and at the mine itself (and there
To wait three days), if Helen had been seen;
Then at the utmost speed to hurry back
Ere seven days ended.   Now he sought the house
Of Conway, who himself had tarried there,
Though late the hour ; but Dennell first would meet
Sylvia.   To her he said, he had been moved
Most strangely by a something he had seen,
Which yet he could not tell ; she must believe
It was not aught that caused him shame to see.
And Sylvia answered, she would take it so.
But he pursued, " Sylvia, be not surprised
"If in the week that follows I remain
"At home alone, nor come to visit you
"Till that be ended."   Jealousy and doubt
Fired Sylvia's heart at this ; in wrath she cried,

" O pattern of all lovers ! what means this ?
" Where shall you wander in that lonely week ?
"Or is it but your thoughts that roam so wide ?
" And are you sure that mine will never stray ?
" No, 'tis your liberty, and I am bound.
" What shall I tell my father ?   Yesternight
" He asked me shrewdly, what had been the theme
"Of our discourse together on the hills ;
" I begged him not to question me of aught
"Until to-day.   I must break silence now ;
" Tell me what way to answer."   Dennell said,
" It is most needful, Sylvia, what I ask.
"Hereafter you shall know the cause ; but now
"I must be silent.   For your father, we
" Will answer him together, how I asked
"Your promise, and you gave it."   " Be it so,"
Sylvia replied ; "but till the week be o'er,
" I hold you not as bound to me at all."
But Dennell, " Nay, I bind thee not."   Therewith
They went to Conway, who, perplexed, perturbed,
Fell into anger not unpardonable,
But closing Dennell's heart ; which else perchance
Had given its secret to a milder touch.
And lastly, Conway threw a challenge thus :
"Assure me this, I claim it as a right,
" You will not use these days for any deed.
" Save such as is already known to me.
But Dennell, " No.   I promise this alone :
" I will not use these days for any deed
" That shall remain untold, the week once o'er."

Conway, though somewhat loth, agreed to this.
With anxious hearts they took their several ways ;
But Conway, coming to his office, found
A letter, that for weighty needs desired
His presence in a town remote from thence
A two days' journey ; so he hastened home
To Sylvia, who at such a time deplored
Her lack of him, entreating his return
At latest on the day when Dennell's week
Of solitude should end.   The father gave
Undoubting promise, and set forth that hour.

But Helen, on the morrow of the day
Whereon she changed the swelling deep for land,
Arose refreshed from sleep ; and when the sun
Was past his heat, she set upon her way,
Bearing a letter that commended her
To Conway, written by her kindly host.
Now presently there passed her two that spoke
The English tongue ; along her side they went
A little space, the nearer of the twain
A comely woman (Laura Farquhar this,
Her husband with her) ; Helen turned and said,
" Lives there a merchant, Conway named, this way ? "
" Thither," said Laura, " we are sped." And so
Walking together, they conversed, and learnt
Each others' names ; and Laura questioned thus ;
" Know you the merchant we are seeking now ? "
" I bear a letter that will make me known,"
Helen replied ; then Laura, " There is none

" More worthy to be trusted.   Years have passed
" Six, and the seventh is passing, since the day
" When first we saw him, on the ship that bore
" Ourselves and him to Rio ; with him went
" His daughter Sylvia.   Then for two years' space
" We met them often, but not since at all,
" For we have lived far off.   But may I learn,
" Is Rio, then, your home ? "

                      But Helen, " No ;
" It is on call of duty I am come.
" Three months ago I had a father still ;
" But by the Baltic wave his spirit passed
" Into the hidden realms ; I closed his eyes.
" While yet his hour of death delayed, and I
" Stood weeping by him, he disclosed a thing
" That much concerned me in this distant land ;
" Conway, and he alone, can help therein."
Laura made answer, " He will help you well.
" But know you none in all the city else ? "
Then Helen named her host, and afterwards
Added, " I was familiar long ago
" With one that lived in Rio some time since ;
" I know not if he still is here to-day.
" His name is Henry Dennell."   Laura cried,
" Him also have we seen ; he sailed with us
" In that same voyage."   Farquhar also spoke :
" Ay, and with Conway he is joined, unless
" Some newer life have taken him since then ;
" Peranne so told us twenty months ago."
And Helen felt a thrill of growing hope.

Now, while they paced the ocean-rippled strand,
Conversing thus together, Sylvia sat
And pondered in her chamber bitterly ;
"'Tis of a piece with all my life that I
"Should suffer this affront in such an hour
" As is a woman's crown of days.   Alas !
" Him I must love, who scorns me thus.

       " What sight

" Was that which troubled Dennell ?   Can I rest
" In trustful ignorance ?   'Twas strange indeed !
" His struggling lips were chained and white ; a groan
" Burst from his choking breast, and yet was stilled ;
" His eyes were fixed on the mere void, it seemed,
" Unless it were a ship's white sail afar
" Skimming the bay ; but I remember now
" I heard (or do I fancy?) a footfall sound
" Upon the path, just ere I turned to look.
" Yet of what import could that be ?   If e'er
" Phantom or ghost did pierce the heart of man,
" Then would I say that Dennell yesterday
" Felt such a terror.   I will watch and wait,
" For I believe him honest, as he says ;
" But wedded wife to him I ne'er will be,
" If in his breast he nurtures and conceals
" This darkling birth of rude tempestuous pangs."

Now on her musings broke the three that came
Out of the city by the winding shore,
Farquhar and Laura and Helen ; and the two
With whom she erst had voyaged greeted her

With cordial voice and clasp of hand, and she
Answered with equal warmth.   They told the cause
That brought them unto Rio ; but the wife
Named not the tenderer tale she bore from him
Who faithful waited in the northern land.
Then, sitting where the trees cast thickest shade
(For thither Sylvia led them), Helen asked
If Conway were at hand ; but Sylvia said,
" My father has been called, three hours ago,
" Through sudden summons hence ; by this day week
" He promised me he surely would return.
" Only, I fear, for you the time is long."
" So long," said Helen, " I am free to stay
" In Rio ; " and she placed in Sylvia's hand
The letter that she bore.   But Helen now
Feared that the time indeed was overlong,
If Dennell were perchance no longer here ;
So presently she questioned thus again :
" I learn that one, who was my friend of old,
" Was with your father twenty months ago.
" His name is Harry Dennell ; can you say,
" Lives he in Rio ?   Does he prosper still ? "
But Sylvia looked with swift and wondering eyes
On her that spoke the name which then, even then,
Vibrated through the currents of her mind ;
She looked, and saw how fair the questioner.
A sudden thought upon her flashed, and bred
A thousand varied feelings, like the hues
Which, when a storm has swept the hills at eve,
Light up the rainbow-tinted sky, the glens,

And swollen torrents, and high glittering crags—
Jealousy, yet relief; the sense that now
Knowledge was near, the dread to feel it near ;
Then blank recoil, as if she had presumed
On idle fancies ; but at last, resolve
That whatsoe'er might come to pass, herself
With eye and ear should witness it, that nought
Should be devised in darkness to her bane ;
The answer framed itself upon her lips
Quick as the thought : "Come spend with us the hours
" Of evening, on the seventh day from now,
" And Henry Dennell you will find.   I know
" He will not fail us, for he pledged his word ;
"Till then he is beset with cares all day.
" He shares my father's commerce."   Helen gave
Acceptance glad ; then further, " He is changed,
" I doubt not, since I saw him ; he was then
"Just entering manhood ; beardless ; quick in speech,
" Motion, and temper ; is he so to-day ?
" Was he not set in fiery peril once
" And almost slain ? "   Then Sylvia, " Yes, 'tis so ;
" A scar upon his brow and temple shows
" Where he was wounded in the burning mine.
" Bearded he is ; for character, yourself
" Shall see and judge.   In all a merchant's ways
" Men deem him skilful."   Farquhar hereupon
Broke into speech abruptly : " Has he ta'en
" A wife ? or does his purpose lie that way ? "
" Nay," answered Sylvia, " married he is not ;
" But if he purpose marrying, none can tell ;

" Least of all men he shows his secret soul."
And Helen heard, and inwardly was glad,
" Secret he is to others, not to me."
And after this she put no question more,
But either listening to the converse round,
Or with brief answer, if there needed such,
Or silent yielding to her gentle thoughts,
Rested in peace ; and then the three returned
Along the shore, while darkness grew apace.

Laura to Sylvia of Peranne that day
Had spoken in the garden.   Sylvia's cheeks
Had flushed with colour, Laura marked it well ;
A tremor glanced across her lips ; she asked
Much of his welfare, and with pleasure heard
What Laura told.   But Clara then drew near,
And Sylvia ceased.   And Laura thought she knew,
But knew not, all that was in Sylvia's mind.
So Laura was determined in herself,
And came another day.   Beneath the cliff
Along the solitary shore they went ;
And there did Laura place in Sylvia's hand
A letter ; Sylvia turned to weakness then.
With trembling fingers scarce she broke the seal ;
And then she sat upon a stone hard by ;
And then she saw the words, and saw beneath
His name that wrote ; she saw and saw them not,
For faintness came upon her.   Laura ran,
And gathered in her hand the salt sea wave,
Bathed the pale brow of Sylvia, till the strength

Of her that was so weak revived again.
She rose and cried, "O help me!"   Laura then,
"What fault, O tell me, has been mine to-day?
"Why are you moved? what is your need of help?
"For I would try my succour if I knew."
And Sylvia answered, "Promise me, I pray,
"Never to tell my weakness in this hour."
And Laura said, "I promise.   Yet the cause—
"Is it so well to hide it?   But perhaps
"You will reveal it to another ear."
Sylvia replied, "To none upon the earth."
But soon again, "O how it dazzles me!
"This way and that the rays of some wild light
"Hover before me.   Who shall answer me?"
And Laura walked in silence.   Sylvia turned
Once more, and cried, "O Laura Farquhar, pledge
"Your promise truly; give me here your hand,
"Both hands, and look upon my eyes, and say,
"You will not fail, when Tuesday's sun declines
"Down towards the mountains of the western verge,
"Ay, a full hour before his orb shall sink,
"To visit me within my father's house.
"It may be, I shall tell you then the cause;
"It may be, not."   And Laura wondering placed
"Both hands in Sylvia's, looked her in the face;
"Most surely do I promise you," she said,
"Not to be wanting at the appointed hour."
And presently they parted.
                              Sylvia ran
Unto her chamber, closed the door, and set

Before her eyes the letter Laura gave,
And sighed, and looked upon the words therein.
"Sylvia, I love you, and have ever loved.
"She who will bear this letter to your hand
"Will tell you, I have prospered well, and thrive
"In the world's sight.   O Sylvia, be my wife.
"If this may be, then the long pang will cease
"Of all that I have suffered all my days.
"If not, with courage I will bear the end
"Which has been destined me.   Your own Peranne."

Seven days, each hour that duty suffered him,
Dennell pursued the search ; but froward fate
Hindered ; for never, as it seemed, the strain
Of various labour so had urged before ;
And Conway's absence caused the whole to weigh
On Dennell's shoulders.   Tuesday's dawn arrived,
Last of the seven, and Helen was unfound ;
Now from the mine the messenger returned,
Saying, nor there, nor on the road at all
Was any trace.   Then Dennell made his way
Down to the harbour ; there inquiring learnt,
An English lady, ere the last week's end,
By ship had ta'en departure.   Could it be
That this was Helen ?   Dennell, hearing all,
Judged so indeed.   Noon came and passed, and still
The hours wore on (and Dennell all the day,
Unfit from agitation of his heart
For daily labour, had remained aloof) ;
He murmured thus :
                    " 'Tis vain ; and hope is o'er.

" Surely she was in Rio for my sake,
" And could have found me, had she willed, ere now.
" But she is gone, and wherefore?   Ah, I guess
" At last the cause—'tis Sylvia.   Fatal hour,
" When with my lips I slew my happiness !
" And coward I, to let occasion pass !
" Helen, my Helen, could I see thy face,
" Nor give one sign, one word?   O mine no more ;
" Does she despise me ?   Nay, if she herself
" Bent to her father's will, as he affirmed,
" I have not done her wrong.   Ah no, I see
" The truth ; it is myself that I have harmed ;
" Is not the goodliest hope, the sweetest flower,
" The branch that was so grafted into me
" I thought it was my own, my very self,
" Imagination's dearest thought, that has
" Sustained me through so many weary hours,
" And twined itself in memory, feeling, life,
" So that I cannot turn to any page
" Of that past record, but I read therein
" Helen ! inscribed, and Helen ! is not this
" Reft from me, torn away, a fragment now
" Of idle fancy, to dissolve and pass
" As a mere day-dream, or poor floweret, cut
" To be an evening's ornament, then thrown
" Into the dust?   Alas ! but plaints are vain ;
" Unmanly are these tears."

                         The hour had come ;
He must depart.   He paused, then spoke again :
" I thought some lightning stroke would pierce the
     clouds

"That hang around me; I had welcomed it,
" E'en though it pierced myself. That shall not be.
" In vain I look for joy, in vain for grief;
" All, all is dead to me. So do I deem
" That many a man in quiet dull content
" Griefless and joyless spends the days of life.
" Yet must I scan this barren scene, and ask
" What first and last is in it. Helen? Ah,
" She is not gone, her memory lingers here;
" I see the elder time yields not so soon
" His rank above the younger. Helen! she
" Was like the sun to me; and now I ask
" Whether she wore that splendour worthily,
" Which in my eyes has ever been so bright.
" I will believe it. Did she truly send
" The message through her father? if 'twere so,
" Then must I say, she did indeed descend
" From the high pinnacle of perfect faith.
" Yet, be it so; my child, though thou didst err,
" I will not yet desert thee in my soul;
" For thine in mine has been involved, and still
" Where'er my guardianship shall o'er thee stretch,
" Most in the secret silence of my thought,
" Or, it may be, in some unfathomed depth,
" Beyond conception, of the future time,
" Thou shalt be sheltered. Never shall rude tongue
" Blame thee within my hearing. Yea, myself
" Can see thy image, and not wholly mourn;
" For now I learn, the expanding flower of life
" Has forms and colours more than I have known;

"And beautiful in days that now are not
"Shall be the bud that ne'er was opened here.
"So do I order that which deepest lies
"Within me.
          "Sylvia? she awaits me now.
"And I must take her as my wife. O how
"Will she, will Conway, hear, when I confess
"All I have thought, and hoped, and done? Confess!
"To seek for Helen, was it then a sin?
"It is my glory; nay, since even yet,
"For all that's come, proof is not absolute
"But Helen may remain in Rio still,
"Sick, hurt perchance; and Conway, of all men,
"Can best discover if 'tis so or not;
"Who shall deny my right to ask his aid,
"For firm conviction in so dear a thing?
"That will I do.
          "The world moves on, howe'er
"This thing or that befalls us. Come, I'll take
"Courage of heart; what things behind me lie
"May ripen, if they ripen, in such hour
"As is ordained by the high will Divine
"That governs all; new paths henceforth are mine."

Now Sylvia waited on the garden lawn.
And Laura came the first, while yet the day
Wanted an hour to eventide; and next
Helen; and silence lay upon the three:
And Laura marvelled, but refrained herself.
But Sylvia's mien was loftier than her wont,

And in her eyes a glowing tender light
Shone, as she greeted each in turn of those
That came invited; and her father now
With Farquhar entered, for upon the road
They met, and loudly rang, while yet afar,
Their voices as in jovial merriment;
And Conway greeted Helen, deeming her
The friend of Laura Farquhar; after these,
Came Clara from the house, released at last
From busy cares; but Dennell came not yet.
And Conway cried, "Why lingers Dennell now?"
And Helen trembled as she heard the name
Familiarly spoken; and she thought,
"This sound is as the breaking of a dream."
And lo! she looked, and at the garden gate
Was Harry Dennell.   Then, a moment's space,
She marked in him the change from youth to man;
The bearded face, the resolute air, the scar
Where he was wounded in the burning mine:
But not for long; for at his entering in
He saw and knew her, and drew near and stood
Before her; and he glanced an instant down,
And knew she wore not on her hand the sign
That marks a wife: the others sat amazed
Beholding him, such pale astonishment
Looked through his eyes.   But now he turned, and saw
That Sylvia pierced his thoughts; such fire had lit
Her eyes, that flashed defiance on him there
(For still she felt a sting, as scorned by him);
An agitating passion seized him then,

And quick resolve; with stern command he spoke;
" What have you done?   Sylvia, I charge you, speak."
Swiftly did Sylvia send the answer back :
" What have I done? all you that hear me now,
" Judge of our cause, which of us two has right
" To stand accuser.   'Tis eight days from now,
" He made entreaty, I should be his wife;
" And to my shame I did consent thereto;
" Was it not just I should expect from him
" Kindness and courtesy?   I say not, love;
" For it may be that lay not in his power.
" Now will I tell exact in every point
" The very truth; consent had scarcely gone
" Out of my lips, he sent me from his side;
" And the next day forbade me name our bond ;
" And till this hour he has not seen me since.
" Now you are witness, now that he returns,
" How harsh his bearing toward me, how he seeks
" Before your face to render me despised."
Then Helen rose all pale, and moved a step,
And spoke : " I was mistaken, well I see,
" In coming hither, being a stranger here;
" These private differences should be composed
" Among yourselves."   And fain was she to go;
But Dennell looked at her, one word he said;
" Helen !"   She stayed her foot, and he pursued;
" Helen, this hour my right remains to speak;
" Though ne'er perchance hereafter, yet this hour.
" It is not now that I can summon back
" Unto your memory or my own the words,

" The scene,.the pledge, of years so long ago,
" Howe'er they are engraven in my soul;
" One question only must I ask of you;
" As now we stand before the eyes of God,
" Be not ashamed; for I myself declare
" I reckon no offence in anywise
" Pertaining to you; you are clear of blame :
" Say truly, then, if ever you declined
" Or did retract the pledge you gave me once?"
" Never," said Helen, " never did I so.
" But you, it seems, have given another pledge,
" Annulling that you gave me." " Ah!" he cried,
" Yourself must surely know his name that spoke
" Untruly, saying you drew back from me."
But Conway now with angry speech broke in :
" This passes all endurance! you commit
" A wrong with every word; if I were young,
" You would not dare it; nor without reproof,
" Though I am aged, shall you trespass now.
" What meant you, when you sought my daughter's hand?
" Freely and unconstrained you pledged yourself;
" Mean you to keep your promise? yea or no?"
Then Dennell answered : " You have made reproach
" Sternly against me. Truly, sir, I own
" 'Tis merited in this, because I failed
" To make you partner of my thought and will
" A week ago; your kindness has been great
" In my concerns; by haste I was misled.
" But for the question you have asked of me
" Thereto I plainly answer. Not by me

"The promise has been broken, which I gave
"Your daughter; yet 'tis broken. Sylvia, hear ;
"Though you condemn me, listen; I must say
"What strange events have brought me to this end."
He paused, and looked at Sylvia ; for her tears
Were flowing through her interwoven hands
That hid her eyes ; then Conway once again :
"What need of speech? the end is plain to see.
"You have ta'en back your promise. Spare our ears
"From hearing explanation of your act."
"I speak to Sylvia," Dennell answering said ;
"Sylvia, there is a tale that I must tell ;
"Condemn me after hearing, if you will ;
"The truth is yet untold. If e'er I seemed
"In word or act discourteous, 'twas in stress
"Of present suffering; pardon me such fault."
Then Sylvia laid aside her hands, and showed
Her face bedewed with tears ; she turned her eyes
On Dennell, saying, "Speak, and I will hear."
And Dennell spoke. "Seven summers ere to-day,
"Helen Dundas was joined to me in troth.
"And never since that hour has true intent
"Been in her heart or mine, to make that pledge
"Of none effect between us. Helen, say,
"Is it not so? and plainly I must ask ;
"Your father claimed, that with your cognizance
"And full concurrence of your mind and heart,
"He wrote to me this wise : you had resigned,
"He said, all hope of marriage with myself ;
"You were obedient to his word and will ;

" And as to stamp his meaning, he affirmed
" You sent me such a message, as a friend
" Might send to friend.   Three years ago he wrote.
" Had he no sanction, no authority,
" Given by yourself? knew you he wrote at all?"
Then, pale as death, and weeping, she replied :
" It is most true, I knew it not.   I held
" As certain, you had perished in the mine.
" But three months since, my father dying told
" The very truth ; and afterwards I learnt
" You sought for me ; and therefore am I come."
Then Dennell : " Ah, I sought for you indeed !
" O Sylvia, you have heard ; not knowingly
" Have I deceived you ; neither have I scorned
" The hand you gave me ; but an elder pledge
" Demands fulfilment.   Truly did I toil
" For her who now has found me ; through deceit
" And strange mischance, not soon nor easily,
" Despaired I of the light of all my life.
" O say I sin not now in claiming her,
" Who has been thus restored."   He ceased ; and all
Looked upon Sylvia ; but the maiden sat
In musing silence lost ; and Conway's brow
Was stern and lowering still ; at last she rose,
In mien and tone and accent so diverse
From that she seemed before, you would have deemed
Another maiden in her stead was there.
Gently she touched her father, gently spoke ;
" Stay but a moment, father ; and you all,
" Delay debate, while Laura goes with me ;

"For she can counsel me in this distress."
But Conway, with surprise and discontent,
Answered, "Ay, go; and has your father, then,
"No share in giving counsel to his child?"
"Surely," she said, "the chiefest share is yours;
"Trust me 'tis so: but now there is a word
"Laura alone, and not myself, can say;
"To you it must be said, and judgment lies
"With you alone." "Go then," in kindlier tone
He answered. So they went apart, and talked
Beneath the trees; and plain it was to see
How earnest was their converse, though unheard
Dennell the while lifted his eyes and caught
The silent tender glance of her so long
Denied to him, and sundered from his sight;
Yea, even yet they stood apart, nor dared
Gladden each other with a mutual smile
Or clasp of hands; only within their eyes
A dawn of hope was rising, faint but clear:
As when a traveller, on an Alpine peak
With hard endurance scaled through nightly hours,
Beholds upon the eastern verge a line
Of glimmering light, first herald of the day;
So Helen now and Dennell felt the beam,
Prophetic token of their long night's end.
But Laura came with Sylvia; first of these
Sylvia began: "I know not if myself
"Can judge of Henry Dennell, but in truth,
"Father, I feel no anger. It is strange
"How this has happened. O be kind, I pray,

" In that which Laura now will say for me."
Conway with brief sign answered; then to him
Thus Laura : " There is one who sailed with us
" Long time ago ; who came to trouble here,
" Yet not dishonourably ; who is now
" Esteemed and prosperous in the northern land—
" Edward Peranne.   He, through myself, has sent
" A letter, asking for your daughter's hand ;
" And she would fain consent, if you allow ;
" She asks that I thus far should plead for him,
" Because my husband and myself alone
" Know him this present hour."   But Conway frowned ;
" Why, Sylvia, he is full of vain conceits ! "
Then Laura : " Nay ; I know not how he seemed ;
" But faithful he has been in heart and soul
" For many years to Sylvia ; for her sake
" Resigned his native land, and all his hope
" Of fortune there and honour, that his name
" Might show without a stain in Sylvia's eyes.
" There is no man of better faculty
" To guide himself to-day."   And Sylvia placed
The moving tender words Peranne had sent
Within her father's hand.   He pondered long ;
And while he pondered, Dennell raised again
His eyes to Helen ; and he saw her lips
Parted and trembling, and it seemed the tears
Lay not far off her eyes, though tears of joy ;
He nearer drew, and said, " Forgive."   But she,
Glancing on Conway, answered with a smile :
" Does not the fortune of your Sylvia stand

T 3

" E'en now in peril ? "   Dennell turned at this
Quickly to Conway, saying, " Sir, Peranne
" Is true and honest."   Conway almost laughed ;
" True, and you have no interest of your own
" To prove it so."   But Dennell : " Long ago
" I gave you proof of this, which you believed."
Then Conway turned to Sylvia : " If you will,
" Send for Peranne, that I may see myself
" How shows his manner at the present time."
And Sylvia took her father's hand, and kissed
His forehead and his lips.   But Helen's tears
O'erflowed ; she took both Dennell's hands in hers ;
He kissed her then.   And Conway cried again,
" Dennell, if I was moved to bitter speech
" By that which seemed a wrong, yet suffer me,
" Since such fair promise has been won at last,
" To say, the maiden of your choice excels
" All that I fancied, when you spoke of her
" In olden days.   Forget not in your thoughts
" Hereafter, how I helped you to this end,
" Ay, more than once ; your joy is mine herein."
And Dennell answered, " I have thought of you
" Ever as one of kindliest will and deed
" Towards me, and in after days still more
" My heart is yours : for saving by your aid,
" Fortune had been too hard for me till now."
And Dennell then with Helen turned and spoke
To Sylvia.   Brief, but from the heart, the words
Uttered on either side.   Then Clara called :
" Know you not that the evening darkens in ?

"You ask not what I think of these affairs ;
"So I had best be silent ; they will move,
"Will I or nill I, as it pleases them.
"So settle all to your content, I pray ;
"But hasten when 'tis over ; for the lights
"Gleam from the window, and 'tis supper-time."
And Conway ; "Yes, our tragic scene is o'er.
"Our hearts are moved to gladness, and 'tis meet
"To pledge the victors, who with loving tie
"Of fourfold hearts have conquered stubborn fate."
But Dennell looked on Helen ; and her eyes
Were raised to his ; he took her yielded hand ;
So from the rest apart they went, and merged
Into the shadow of the twilight trees.

EPITHALAMIUM.

Sweetly from heaven
    Springeth the light ;
They who were driven
    Darkly through night,
Lovers true-hearted,
Stormily parted,
    Lost and astray,
How, reunited,
Tenderly plighted,
    Breathe they to-day !

Wept they for sorrow,
  Weep they for joy,
Morrow on morrow
  Never can cloy.
Hear their devotion,
Earth, air, and ocean !
  Now do they prove
Perfect the vision,
Winning fruition
  Sacred of love.

All their sweet blisses
  Who shall declare ?
Dwell in their kisses
  Mysteries rare ;
Hope overflowing,
Memory glowing
  Soft as a star,
Fruits ever healing,
Lightnings revealing
  Vistas afar.

All now is righted,
  Trespass and wrong ;
Truth, that united,
  Leads them along.
Pausing, delaying,
Silently praying,
  Turn they aside,

Turn from the living,
Gently forgiving
  Him who has died.

See where, around them
  Thronging the way,
Friendship has crowned them
  Laughing and gay.
Who but rejoices?
Hear the glad voices
  Ringing ascend ;
" Brave was their striving,
" Now be their thriving
  " Blithe to the end ! "

Ah, and another
  Spirit long-tried,
Brother with brother,
  Walks by the side.
Thou too, O lover,
Soon wilt discover
  All that of old
Lured thee unsleeping,
Sighing and weeping—
  Treasures untold.

Now with her queenly
  Golden array
Nature serenely
  Girdles the day.

Over the mountains
From the sun-fountains,
　Over the tide,
Colours are streaming;
Lo! in their gleaming
　Bridegroom and bride.

Earth! by thy numberless
　Valleys so fair:
Heaven! by the slumberless
　Wings of the air;
By thy free motion,
Life-breathing Ocean,
　Cherish, we pray,
These whom a token
Ne'er to be broken
　Mingles to-day.

From their embraces
　Children be born
Fair with all graces
　Fresh as the morn!
Ye that above us
Foster and love us,
　Spirits on high,
Keep and defend them,
Aid and befriend them
　Ever and aye!

THE END.